WARPAINT

J.J. MAYA

SOCCIONES

ISBN: 978-1-5272-5906-5

Cover Illustration© by Stephen McDermott

Cover design & typesetting by Socciones Editoria Digitale

www.socciones.co.uk

To my Stevie, Joe & Jamie.

CONTENTS

1

PRIMER

Karen Carpenter sang "We've only just begun," as the hired limousine pulled into priority parking at Glasgow Airport.

"Mrs. Campbell and Mr. Delgado, congratulations! I've reserved seats 2a and 2c. Please go to gate 12 where your flight will soon be boarding."

Rick and I locked eyes as the economy class passengers looked on.

I could get used to this, I thought as I smiled at a young woman who was watching me from behind the cordoned off area. As I strode proudly into the First-Class Lounge on the arm of my new American husband, I gazed at the assistant who was serving complimentary drinks to the passengers awaiting the call for their flight. It was a well-known fact that they liked to turn up for boarding at the very last minute to avoid the others who would be sitting down the back in economy. Her manicured hand trembled slightly as she poured two glasses of celebratory champagne. I noticed that Rick held her gaze a moment too long for my liking.

Once airborne, and the first service of the flight had been completed, I reclined in the leather seat and took my yellow book out for a quick read.

"What's that you're reading?" Rick asked, twisting the light switch above his head.

"Only the book that brought us together." I ran my fingertip lovingly across the title, feeling at once happy and relieved.

"Not that garbage again!" Rick stopped playing with the switch and turned to look at me. "You really believe in all that stuff, don't ya?" I noticed the light above his head appeared to illuminate brighter, casting an almost angelic glow over the two of us.

"If it wasn't for this garbage, you wouldn't be sitting in First-Class with me now, would you?" Cheeky git! I thought, as the light above us bounced off my diamond wedding ring and flashed across the aircraft ceiling. Rick and I exchanged glances. I was sick of him calling my book 'garbage' and on this special day—our wedding day—I wasn't prepared to let it go.

Sensing my discomfort, Rick mumbled under his breath, "S'pose you got a point." He took the yellow book from my grasp and let it fall casually to the cabin floor. Leaning in for a kiss, I didn't protest. I'm sure the stewardess with the broad, red-painted smile had seen it all before.

***

We had met just six weeks earlier in the department store where I worked as an account manager for a leading beauty brand. Rick had walked towards me, full of swagger and self-confidence and asked me for directions to the Hermes Counter. From his accent, I guessed he was an east coast American. My ear had become tuned to years of watching the Housewives of New York City. I had sent him off in the direction of the counter before taking the opportunity to take a quick read of the yellow book. I hid it under a pile of paperwork making sure to keep it well under wraps. I opened at a new chapter and read the words, "Taking a chance is the first step on the ladder of success." The words flitted in and out of my mind as I had drifted into a reverie, recalling past memories. Wracking my brain, I tried to think of times when I had taken a chance, but to my annoyance I couldn't think of anything that stood out from my childhood. Moments passed… I looked up to see the same man staring at me, the American. He had returned.

"Did you find what you were looking for?" I asked.

"I have now," he replied, his brown eyes glinting wickedly.

It was instant attraction. When he asked if I wanted to go for a coffee after work, I shook off my normally shy demeanour and found the courage to say 'yes.'

The rest, as they say, is history.

***

The flight passed quickly, hurtling me towards my new life in New York City. The thought was both immensely exhilarating and oddly frightening at the same time. Rick sat by my side, snoring. Loudly. Everything would be fine for him. He was returning home to the life that he had left behind only six weeks ago. I gazed at the outline of his face. His tanned skin bore some little indentations and pock marks left over from his teenage years, but overall, he was wearing well. He told me he was 35 years old, a fact authenticated by his Fed-Exed birth certificate. (I had no reason not to believe him, although I had occasionally caught myself wondering why such a good-looking man was still single and childless.)

I banished that thought to the back of my mind as I became aware that the other passengers in the cabin were looking over at us. Rick's snoring had become noticeably louder. I felt my cheeks flush with embarrassment as I realized that the potent mix of being newly married and consuming four Tanqueray Gins at an altitude of 30,000 feet had proved a little too much for my new husband.

As we flew ever closer to our destination, I began to think about my own situation; there I was, living alone in a rented flat in the west end of Glasgow My parents had died in a car crash when I was just eight years old, leaving me to bear the full brunt of years in foster care. It had been a miserable existence as I was shunted from family to family and from pillar to post, hoping that some day a loving family would adopt me…it never happened.

Rick's surprise marriage proposal had shaken me to the core, but I hadn't needed to think twice. In the short time I had known him, he had proven himself to be one big surprise that I just couldn't let go of.

As expected, everyone I spoke to had an opinion, most of them negative. A few of my colleagues told me I was crazy to be leaving Glasgow behind to jet off into the sunset with a man I barely knew. Deep down, I knew they were all wrong.

I'd like to see them in my position…would they have said no? I don't bloody think so!

A creeping thought snuck into my frontal lobe *most people would have given it more time, Willow.* I shrugged it off and took another sip of the bubbling champagne. *Too late now!*

Not surprisingly, my flat-mate, Geneviève, had the most to say about my imminent departure.

"You can't go off and leave me; what the hell am I going to do?" or "This is all the thanks I get for renting you a room? Now what am I going to do?" She couldn't have cared less about my happiness; all she could think of was herself. Geneviève was the 'pretty one.' The one who always got what she wanted when we went clubbing. Now, she would have to find someone else to be her wing woman

I had made up my mind. No-one would have been able to change it. I was about to fly the nest, and no-one was going to stop me.

Rick's snores grew louder, to the annoyance of our fellow first-class passengers who, like us, were flying on the business expense account. Looking around me, I felt like an outsider. I bet that not one of these privileged, entitled passengers had ever had to think about how they would scrape together enough money to buy a sandwich for lunch. Now, my life was about to change for the better!

What had surprised me the most about our whirlwind wedding had been Rick's 'no expense spared' attitude towards getting me whatever I needed. Every purchase had been put on his credit card. He flashed it at every opportunity. It was black. One of the girls on the shop floor told me she had seen that type of card before and that it was very exclusive. Only a few managed to obtain one. I remember how she had looked at me when she said that. She looked like she wanted to be me. It was the first time in my life that I realised someone wanted to be me. Willow Campbell, pushing 33, slightly plump for my 5ft 7 and three quarters of an inch frame. Facial features scarred by a brush with a basal cell carcinoma. But looking on the positive side of life I had acquired an inherent skill for making myself look borderline glamorous. I was a skilled makeup artist who had learned every trick in the book over my eight-year long career working behind cosmetics counters in stores all around the Glasgow area.

Looking over at Rick, I felt a wave of relief wash over me. Here was a man who loved me so much that he was willing to propose after such a short time. And here I was, finally finding myself ready to embark on this huge commitment called 'marriage' without even giving it so much as a second thought. The unhappy cloud that had been hanging over me for such a long time had finally been banished to wherever it was that unhappy clouds came from. Now, when I looked up at the sky, I could finally see the sunshine.

Twenty minutes into our journey through the streets of New York and after what seemed like an age stuck in traffic, our grubby yellow cab with the cracked leather seats pulled up in front of the entrance to a towering brown bricked building in what looked like, to my untrained eyes, an insalubrious part of town. I peered out of the window, then looked over at Rick.

"Is this it?" I asked

Surely not, I thought. No matter how hard I tried, there was no way in hell I could disguise the notes of disappointment in my voice.

"This is it. Home Sweet Home." Rick stared over the top of my head and looked wistfully at his apartment home.

"I thought you said you lived in Manhattan?" I queried, hoping against hopes there had been some dreadful mistake.

Rick grinned from ear to ear, "I do." I followed his gaze as he stared up at an apartment window nearing the top of the building.

He smirked as he pointed to the sign above the entrance to the apartment building 'Manhattan Heights!'

"Home Sweet Home."

Only the 'H' and 'E' were missing, and an 'N' had been crudely spray painted in making the sign read 'Manhattan *N*ights'.

Sucking up my disappointment, I carefully climbed out of the cab, putting my best Repetto Ballet Pump forward, trying not to look how I felt. A blast of ice-cold wind whipped around me, taking my breath away as Rick led the way into the apartment building lobby, dragging two huge suitcases behind him. I followed on behind him, taking everything in at once. As I closed the apartment building door behind me, I saw that much to Rick's annoyance, there was an 'out of order' sign placed across the elevator door.

So, this is why New York women are so skinny, I calculated. *Everything makes perfect sense now.* Thinking I had just come up with the perfect title for a woman's non-fiction book, I was startled out of my thoughts as Rick led me over to a honey coloured wooden bench that was pushed up against the lobby wall.

"Sit your boney ass down over there while I take the cases up...I might be a while; when I get back, we'll go for brunch."

"But Rick, I want to see the apartment." I stared at him squarely on. I hadn't waited all this time to be told I had to wait some more.

Rick smirked, "You'll have all the time in the world to see it, *trust me*, and you don't want to do this climb after a transatlantic flight." Relenting, he put his arms around me, cosseting me it seemed, from all New York City's unpleasantness. "I'll be down in 10."

Huddling under my thin coat, I sat on the lobby bench and leaned against the great expanse of faux marble lining the wall. It was a shame really; my grand entrance in the Big Apple hadn't been the glamorous event I had conjured up in my imagination all these weeks.

As I waited, my mind flicked vigorously over the days preceding our departure and the build up to our big day. The yellow book had had a huge part to play.

***

Twenty minutes later, Rick finally re-appeared, whisking me from my daydream state straight back to the present, red in the face and seriously out of breath.

"Six weeks. That's all it takes. Six weeks in Glasgow and my fitness is gone," he panted, wiping a smattering of dust from his navy-blue pea coat.

"It must have been all those fish suppers washed down with lashings of Irn Bru!" I said, grabbing him around his slightly paunchy waistline. Patting him on the stomach, I smirked, "Or perhaps it was those pineapple cakes from Greggs that did the trick!"

"But look at what I gained," Rick gazed into my eyes, wiping a wisp of brunette hair away, "- a brand new wife!" He planted a kiss squarely on my lips. "Come on, let's go! I've got a lot to show you." Leading me out towards the icy sidewalk, Rick put his two fingers in his mouth and hailed us a cab with the kind of nonchalance that only a native New Yorker could muster.

"Park Avenue, please!" he told the cabbie.

Thirty minutes later, the drama of our arrival soon forgotten, we found ourselves huddled on a rickety bench in front of Cafe on Park Avenue. The chic little cafe had a window display that looked like something straight out of Charlie and The Chocolate Factory, with cupcakes piled high on dainty wire cake stands. I snuggled into the warmth of his neck, inhaling the faint fragrance of cedar and vetiver, as I stood and contemplated the amazing dream-like life I had suddenly found myself walking into. This time though, I, Willow Campbell-Delgado, had the starring role. No more watching from the sidelines, no more hoping, praying and wishing for a better life.

Perfectly located for a spot of people watching, we sipped our ice cold Peroni whilst nibbling on tiny portions of bruschetta, accompanied by dainty bowls of olive tapenade. The citizens of New York City strutted, strolled and jogged past us enroute to their various appointments with their hairdresser, doctor, or personal trainer. A particularly elegant looking woman, dressed in an expensive camel coat, caught my attention. As she strutted confidently towards us, I studied how she kept her balance in those towering heels and admired the bounce in her hair as she walked. *I wonder if this is how I might look after a few months spent as Rick's wife.*

Snapping me abruptly out of my daydream, Rick stood up abruptly and announced, “Be back in five, got to take this call” I sipped the last few dregs of my beer, yawning as the jet lag kicked in. Now, all I could think of was climbing into a huge king-sized bed, and relaxing between crisply laundered Ralph Lauren sheets, before falling into a deeply restful slumber entwined in Rick's arms.

Just as I was about to light my imaginary Jo Malone candle, Rick returned, wearing an expression I had never seen before.

“Em…do you have your credit card on you? Or is it in one of the suitcases?"

Rick looked embarrassed as I rummaged around in my bum bag or 'fanny pack' as the Americans like to call it. I handed the card over to him, feeling relieved that I had managed to clear the balance before leaving for the USA.

As Rick paid the bill, I realized there was a lot I didn't know about my new husband, but I consoled myself that with time on our side, these looks and expressions would soon become second nature to both of us. Of that I was sure. Rick grabbed my hand and pulled my now weary body up out of the spindly chair.

"C'mon babe! You look tired. Let's go home."

Arriving back at 'Manhattan *N*ights' for the second time that day, I prayed inwardly for a small miracle - that the lift would be working. Both Rick and I had been nowhere near a gym since the day we met, and I had the added pounds to prove it. But there was to be no way around it. Fourteen flights later, my legs shook, my head spun, and visible beads of sweat dripped from my forehead. As Rick, who looked like he was in a similar state to me, went to put his key in the door, it took all my might to find the necessary breath to stop him.

"Just a minute!" I gasped, holding onto my knees as I looked down at my swollen ankles, "Wait a wee minute."

Rick took the key out of the lock and shot me an exasperated look.

Squaring up to him, I placed my hands on my hips and breathing heavily exhaled loudly, "Well? Aren't you going to?"

"Aren't I gonna what, for Chrissakes?"

I felt my face fall. *How could he possibly* ***not*** *know what I want?*

"Carry me over the threshold?"

Thick, damp-filled air hung heavily around us as I awaited his answer. Rick frowned as he registered what I was asking him to do. Then he looked me up and down like a physicist making a complicated calculation before deciding whether to go ahead with the experiment. It was evident from his body language that he thought I was too fat to be picked up.

He erupted, slamming the side of the door with the palm of his hand, as biting peals of laughter rang out of him.

Cheeky git! How dare he? I've been on Weightwatchers for the past month!

"What's so funny?" I asked, grim-faced, sucking in my abs for good effect.

"You gotta be joking me, Willow!" he gasped, trying to straighten his face into a serious looking expression.

Silence.

"You're not joking, are you?" He cocked one eyebrow as he attempted to regain his composure, but I could tell another rolling bout of laughter was threatening to erupt.

"Christ almighty, Rick! Isn't this what every woman wants?" Now it was my turn to second-guess myself. *Isn't this what every woman wants, or have I just been watching too many romantic movies?*

Finally registering the look of disappointment on my face, Rick took a step towards me, then, catching me by surprise, scooped me up. *That's more like it!*

The walls swayed as Rick staggered one step forward then two faster steps back, "Jesus! Willow!"

"Whoa there! Steady!" I screamed hysterically as we lolled from side to side like a ship at sea navigating the swells of the ocean. Regaining his balance, and holding his collection of mail in his mouth, Rick somehow managed to put the key in the door and open it while I held on tightly with my arms around his neck, secretly loving the absolute romance of it all. *I don't care what anyone thinks of me! I'm having the time of my life!*

Deciding it best to help him out, I reached my hand out in the darkness and flicked on the light switch at once illuminating, the apartment and our faces, as the hallway strip lighting sprung into life.

I scanned the view in front of me with bated breath.

A huge surge of disappointment swept over me (and not for the first time that day) as a noxious smell of stale cigarette smoke and cheap booze filled the atmosphere. The fumes brought back the memory of arriving at Geneviève's flat and opening the door to be greeted by a similar assault on my senses. To make it worse, a musty smell permeated the atmosphere.

Visibly crushed by my look of disappointment, Rick rushed towards the windows, pulling open the blinds, "I'll open the windows...let some air in."

Just then, my nostrils were filled with a waft of thick, cold, pungent New York City air, flowing in through the open window. I shivered.

Walking slowly around the tiny apartment, which was little more than a room and kitchen with a bedroom off to the side, I ran my finger along the sideboard, picking up a thick line of dust. The apartment had clearly not been cleaned the whole time that Rick was away. Bang went my vision of housecleaners coming in. Catching Rick's eye, I felt sorry for him. I knew he could register my look of disappointment and I felt strangely bad for him. It was time to bring out the big guns and turn this situation around. Making a dire attempt at being the playful new wife, I winked at him, "Could do with a woman's touch, Ricky boy."

Rick blushed slightly. My heart melted. Realising that this was probably not how he had envisaged bringing home his new wife, I snuggled up to him, putting my arms once again around his warm neck.

"Where's the bedroom?"

"Now you're talking!"

Rick led me by the hand towards the closed door and opened it to reveal the king-sized bed of my dreams. It was gigantic, taking up almost the whole room, and was dressed in pristine white Kate Spade linen. *Result! This man clearly has taste.* Throwing himself down on the bed, Rick pulled me on top of him, caressing my neck, running his hands up and down my spine, reminding me once again that we were, in fact, on our honeymoon. And then it happened. That same familiar sensation I had experienced as we were about to land at JFK; I needed to pee, really bad. Pulling myself out of Rick's clutches, I sat up straight and crossed my legs, hoping I would make it in time.

"Where's the bathroom?" I asked.

"In there," Rick pointed to a door facing onto the side of the bed.

Relieved it was so close, I rushed over, "En-suite?" I enquired, flashing a mischievous smile full of promise.

"Luxury as standard."

Closing the door swiftly behind me and throwing myself ungraciously onto the cold seat, I was stopped in mid-flow by the sight of a huge scrawl written in red lipstick over the vanity mirror - "Call Me!"

"What the f...?" Ping went the elastic band chorus in the pit of my stomach.

On closer inspection, I deduced the message was written in Dolce Vita by Dior, a long-lasting luscious red beloved by all makeup artists.

Scanning the tiny room, I found evidence of a woman's presence everywhere I looked: scanty underwear lying at the bottom of the bathtub, an opened box of tampons, and foundation rings on the windowsill. My stomach lurched and my head spun as I took it all in. Whoever had been here, had only just left, that much was certainly evident. Examining further it looked like whoever had been living here was a fan of Agent Provocateur judging by the label sticking out of the lacy red bra which was hanging off the hook on the back of the bathroom door.

Frantically scanning back through our previous conversations, I tried to remember if he had ever spoken about another significant woman in his life.

What the hell have I missed? Alarm bells rang out as I went over our chats and talks that went on long into the night, highlighting our precious evenings together at his serviced apartment in Ingram Street. *Perhaps he has a roommate that he has forgotten to tell me about? Although, what kind of lodger would be making herself at home like this in Rick's en-suite?* Engulfed by a sea of overwhelming thoughts, I sat down heavily on the edge of the tub and held my pounding head in my hands. My stomach lurched the way it used to as I walked onto the shop floor in Devonshire's.

"Willow? Willow? You alright in there?"

Silence. I couldn't bring myself to answer him.

"You haven't fallen asleep on me, have you?"

The knocking grew louder and more urgent as I sank deeper into despair. Rick frantically attempted to open the door from the other side as I watched the door handle go up and down.

"Willow...let me in!" he shouted.

Moments passed. Slowly, I stood up and released the door from the lock, taking a step back as I held the door ajar. Following Rick's gaze from me to the scene around me, I watched as the colour drained from his face, his worried expression at once replaced by a look of utter shock.

Holding aloft a pair of red silk knickers, I stared at Rick.

"Who in hell do these belong to?"

Folding his arms tightly while clearing his throat, Rick's wild-eyed stare had settled slightly as he prepared to launch into an explanation.

"That I can explain."

2

THE SANDMAN

That night, Rick had been banished to the couch in the living room to spend what should have been our first night as a married couple.

I lay in bed alone, perplexed and unsure. My mind raced uncontrollably while my body called out for sleep. *Am I a fool? What's he doing with someone like me anyway?* The previous allure of Rick's king-sized bed had faded and now all it represented was his past, and a life that I would probably never truly know. *Seven years, he goes out with someone for 7 years then dumps her after he meets me? And why am I only just finding this out now? He should have told me before we got married!* I'm sure I must have asked him at some point if he had been in a serious relationship, but Rick had just shrugged and hinted at a string of frivolous relationships which didn't have any significance. Significance? Then what the fuck is 7 years with one person if it isn't significant? Clutching my knees tightly under my chin, I shuddered as the voices ringing in my ears became louder and louder,

"See! Told you! You should have listened to us."

"It's absolute madness going all the way to New York with a man you hardly know."

"You must be off your freakin' head to even contemplate it."

The vision of Greta, my floor manager in the Beauty Hall, peering at me, snorting with self-righteous derision and laughing in my face as I told her I was leaving for America now haunted me. I felt sick to my stomach.

Was she right? Why didn't I think this through? Oh my God, what have I done?

Early the next morning, I awoke to a pounding headache and a streak of crusted drool trailing down the right-hand side of my mouth. Dehydrated from the flight, I leaned over to take a sip of the fresh orange juice that I had brought into the bedroom the previous night. Not yet fully awake, I welcomed the sensation of the juice in my parched mouth, swishing the liquid from one side of my mouth to the other. Then, I bit into something hard.

What the…?

It happened again.

Looking down at the contents of the glass, I couldn't quite believe what I was seeing: a trail of worker ants had climbed up onto the bedside table, circling, and making its way back down again, while a group of the less fortunate ones had formed a thick, dark, nasty layer on the top of my juice.

"Aaaargh!"

I spat into the glass.

"What is it?" Rick rushed in. "What's happened?"

I scowled at the glass of ant infested juice then stared at Rick. The expression on his face twisted and distorted as he made a vain attempt at mock sympathy.

"Welcome to the Big A!" he announced.

"The Big Apple you call it? The freakin big apple?" I spat out black ants as I spoke, wiping them indelicately from the side of my face. "You think this is funny?"

I watched in awe as he exploded into great outbursts of laughter, gripping his sides tightly. I had never seen anyone laugh so hard. *It's not that funny.* He was now bent over, holding onto his knees, as I spat yet another dead ant into the glass. Every time I attempted to speak;

Rick erupted. Obviously, I was the funniest thing he had seen in a long time. Gradually calming down in between howls of laughter, I was able to make out the words "sprayed" and "apartment."

"Sprayed? What do you mean sprayed?" I asked, wiping my mouth on a handkerchief. "You mean toxic chemicals all over the place? And how can ants climb this high up anyway? I don't get it."

Finally calming down, Rick pulled himself together, took out his cell phone from his back pocket and called downstairs to the front desk.

"Hi Tomas, Rick here. Yes, Glasgow was great, thanks." Rick flashed a cocky smile at me, and I could tell he was doing his best not to erupt into another bout of laughter at my expense.

"Looks like since I've been gone, the ants have come back." Turning his back on me, I heard him say in a low voice, "You know Isabella doesn't clean." Thinking I hadn't heard that comment, he turned around to face me once again, flashing another smile then signaling over to me, "Two pm OK for you to let the guys in to spray?"

"Suppose so, what else am I going to be doing, except cleaning this damn apartment?" I replied sulkily, spitting more ants from my mouth, picking them off my pyjama top, the ones I had bought especially for our first 'married' night together. Now the white satin top was dotted with little black things that resembled polka dots.

Rick turned his back on me pretending he didn't hear the disdain in my voice.

"Two pm it is, Tomas. You too. Catch you later."

Looking closer at the carpet, which appeared to be swaying like palm fronds in a Caribbean breeze, I realised the carpet fibres were moving. The whole apartment was well and truly infested. Shuddering, I felt cold spread all the way down my spine as I noticed a trail of the little blighters crawling in and out of my half-opened suitcase.

"Looks like they found the Tunnocks Tea Cakes," I called out, feeling faintly happy that Rick would no longer have his favourite tea cakes to look forward to.

Serves him damn well right.

Rick ran over to check. Peering into the suitcase, he stared back at me and frowned.

"You're right. I was so looking forward to those," he replied, disappointment colouring his voice.

Now it was my turn to laugh as Rick realised there would be no treats to dunk in his tea, if he ever got around to buying a damned kettle. Ignoring me and the situation he was about to leave me in, he looked at his watch.

"Shoot! Is that the time?"

Rick scurried around the bedroom pulling out a clean shirt from his wardrobe. I looked at my phone, it was only 6:30am but it appeared the day started early over here.

"What time do you leave?" I asked, watching him closely as he transformed into the suave version of himself, I had seen that first day in Devonshire. His jet-black hair shone with vitality as he straightened his tie and fixed his starched shirt cuffs. He pulled his leather belt tight, although he did appear to struggle slightly.

"Now," came the rushed reply.

Leaning in for a kiss, on the side of my face that was not covered in crusty ant residue, Rick flicked one of the blighters off my collar bone

"I'll be back for 7pm. Now don't forget, pest control will be here at 2pm. So, make sure you're here to let them in. I've left you a key and five dollars on the kitchen table and a map too."

Rick appeared to stare at me a moment too long, making me feel slightly uncomfortable.

Five dollars? What am I supposed to do with five measly dollars?

Then he was gone, slamming the door noisily behind him. As I swung my legs out of the bed, taking care not to stand on the moving trail of worker ants, the red-lipsticked message on the bathroom mirror screamed at me, unsettling me, reminding me of the previous night's furore. *What kind of fresh hell is this?*

3

GIRL IN A HURRY

As soon as Rick had left, I got up, washed, and brushed my teeth three times before dressing in ten minutes flat. I was faintly glad to be on my own for the first time. I was one of those strange people who liked their own company and relished time alone, if only to re-charge and get ready for the next day.

I surveyed my surroundings while picturing the room layouts in my head. Years of reading Geneviève's collection of interior design magazines had left me with quite a talent for room re-designs and shifting furniture.

I planned on visiting the nearest Ikea at the first opportunity to grab a few things for the apartment. Or maybe I could persuade Rick to go shopping with me in some of New York's outstanding furniture and accessory shops. I knew all the names of these stores by heart and where to find them. I even had an app on my phone which told me which ones I was within walking distance of.

The first thing I would do would be to change out the streamlined sofa for something squishier and more comfortable. *Royal blue velvet...sage green velvet...stately winged armchairs, one for each side of the fireplace...that would be perfect.*

Then I got onto thinking of paint colours before I was snapped out of my interior design daydream by a sudden thirst for a cup of tea. I had been in the USA for two days now, and like a drug addict pines for their line of coke, I was in desperate need of a cup of tea.

Grabbing the five-dollar bill, keys and map from the kitchen table, I threw on the thin winter coat I had arrived in and made a dash for the door.

The air was thick with city smells like the ones I was used to from home; the only difference here was the pungent aroma emanating from the hot dog carts. Deep down I knew it was a smell I would slowly get used to, but, right now, it made me want to be sick.

On and on I walked, passing an interesting array of corner shops, dirty looking dining establishments that made you wonder how they ever got a license to sell food, and cute little vintage stores selling things you would find hard to believe there was ever a market for. There were window displays filled with laundry airers and pull out portable washing lines and crazy looking dryer balls that softened clothes in the drying cycle. And there appeared to be a dry-cleaning establishment on every street corner.

There appears to be some kind of obsession with doing laundry in this city.

As I continued to walk, stopping every now and then to check the map Rick had given me, it dawned on me that I had been walking the streets of Queens for almost an hour. I was dying for a cup of tea and although I had passed countless branches of Starbucks and Italian style coffee shops, I had made it my mission, that first morning, to buy a kettle. A strong cup of brew first thing in the morning would be just the thing to settle my nerves, of that I was sure.

It was only just past 10am but the jet lag had knocked me for six and it felt like the middle of the afternoon. To accomplish my mission, I knew that I would have to find a department store, something akin to the one looming straight ahead: D'Arcy's Department Store.

They would be bound to sell a kettle in there, right? I thought.

Looking through the windows of the stately Art Deco building, I could just about make out the svelte figures of rows and rows of makeup artists dressed head to toe in black uniform. Some wore their hair perfectly coiffed whilst the MAC assistants looked the same way they looked the world over; a complex take on grunge and punk with a splash of eccentricity thrown in for good measure. My heart skipped a beat as I walked through the open door which was carefully guarded by a top hatted elderly door man.

"Hello, Welcome to D'Arcy's Department Store."

The old door man smiled, his eyes twinkling with delight as he beckoned me in. The rough luxe exterior of this Grande dame of a building had seen happier times, and it was obvious that several vain attempts had been made to hide its cracks and flaws. It had this in common with the makeup artists who worked there at least, otherwise known as, what I would call, the mistresses of disguise.

Inside the building I noticed there were visible signs of low-grade maintenance carefully disguised with interior design tricks. Flowing velvet curtains hid unsightly cracks in the paintwork and there had clearly been attempts to mask the damp patches seeping through the walls.

The sea of women dressed in black went about the business of the day: primping, prepping and beguiling clients with their professional stance, demurely painting the faces of the women of Queens, while bystanders complimented their work, suggesting colours and scrutinising techniques. This secret world was familiar to me: a world where women shared their concerns and problems with each other, and the art of disguise possessed the power to either reveal or conceal. I could feel myself getting sucked in as I heard the opening notes of Frank Sinatra's 'Fly Me to the Moon' followed by Tony Bennett singing 'San Francisco.' The music playing in the background only served to make the whole experience, a very special one indeed. My heart leapt with the absolute familiarity of it all, to an onlooker the ease with which I expertly moved about the counters gave me the appearance of a native New Yorker but deep down the nerves I was beginning to feel threatened to disarm me, throwing me into a mild state of panic.

Was I here in New York City, shopping all by myself? What if something were to happen to me? Who would know or even care?

Alarmed by this sudden realisation that I was truly all by myself in the big city, the sensation was both delicious and frightening. I felt a rush of frigid coldness travel up and down my spine as I shivered. Something about this experience reminded me of a time on holiday in Greece, when I had jumped off a yacht into the crystal-clear water below only to be immediately filled with panic as I realised my feet couldn't touch the bottom of the ocean. I stopped for a moment to calm my breathing, soothing myself as I waited for the fleeting moment of panic to disappear.

"Hello love! Welcome to D'Arcy's Department Store."

Jolted out of my thoughts, I looked up to see a tall, young man stare back at me. I had already made up my mind to leave and head back to the safety of the ant-infested apartment, but there was something faintly intriguing about hearing a British accent when I was so far away from home. Comforted by the familiarity of his accent, part of me wanted to learn more about this man and how he came to be standing here in front of me.

"Hello!" I replied warmly, my curiosity getting the better of me.

"Now, don't tell me you're from Glasgow?" the man asked, as he looked down at me.

Shocked that he had pinpointed my accent exactly, I replied, "How did you guess?"

"I trained there for a few weeks before I came out here to work. What was that store called—you know the big glitzy one? The one on Buchanan Street?"

"Devonshire's?"

"That's it! That's the one!" he exclaimed excitedly. Flicking his long dark hair off the side of his face, revealing a sharply contoured chin and chiseled cheekbones. His searing blue eyes glinting under the harsh lights of the store.

"That's my old store! I've just come from there!" I said excitedly, "I arrived yesterday."

"What're the chances, eh? That's bloody amazing, that is!" he smiled.

For a fleeting moment, he looked wistful, his expression taking on a faraway gaze.

"So, what brings you all the way over here?" he asked, bringing himself promptly back to earth.

"A kettle," I replied. "Oh! And a man!" I added on, suddenly feeling stupid for giving away too much information to a stranger.

"I might have known!" he laughed warmly.

"What's so funny?" I asked, wondering what on earth could provoke such a reaction from a stranger.

"Funny? It's the first thing all British expats do the day after they arrive, once they realise there is no way on earth they are going to make tea in a microwave. So, what do they do? They all rush out in search of a kettle." The assistant stopped to take a breath, then carried on, pointing directions, "We have quite a selection on the 4th floor, right next to the elevator, or should I say *lift*?"

Startled by his eerily accurate assessment of me and not knowing what else to say, I stared at my feet, mumbled, "Righty-oh, I'll be off then." Then sped off through the crowd of shoppers.

I made my way towards the lift and pressed the button for 4th floor Electricals. Glancing back, I could see the assistant relaying his recent encounter with me to another assistant. Funny thing is, prior to my arrival in New York, I had never considered myself to be the least bit funny, yet over here, it was a whole different story. A wave of self-consciousness washed over me as it struck me then that there was a lot about living in New York that I was going to have to get used to.

Twenty minutes later and feeling slightly fatigued from the morning's events, I decided to grab a seat in D'Arcy's Cafe and spend a few moments watching the world go by. My mission to buy a kettle had been accomplished and now seemed the appropriate time to relax and rejuvenate over a hot cup of char. Sipping on the hot tea, I retrieved the yellow book from my bag and opened it at the chapter I had been reading the previous evening, when the shit had hit the fan.

"*Believe you are, and you will be.*"

How could so few words mean so much? Could I just close my eyes and believe that here I am in New York and that all is right with me and the world? Or was it all just a crock of shit? Was it just another marketing ploy to lure in gullible human beings like myself who were so down on their luck that they thought things could never change for the better? Yet, here I was, alone and free of the shackles that had been placed around me all my life.

"*Believe you are, and you will be.*"

Could it be possible to just believe who I wanted to be and transform into that person? Surely not.

"Penny for them?"

I opened my eyes to see a familiar pair of beautiful blue eyes staring back at me. Coaxing myself out of my dream-like state, I took a few seconds to realise that the vaguely familiar looking person staring at me was the assistant from the beauty hall, the one who had been laughing at me twenty minutes earlier.

"Well, well, well, if it's not 'the girl in a hurry.' The assistant immediately recognised me. "I see you found the kettles!"

"You don't miss much, do you?" I responded, surprised at this interlude with a stranger.

Unsure of how to proceed with the conversation, I waited. The assistant assumed a serious tone as he leaned in for a closer look at my book. He was tall and thin, but muscular, and had the most amazing physique which was just visible through the thin fabric of his black long-sleeved tee shirt.

"No! Not much gets past these eyes," he declared proudly while pointing at his temples. "It's a fabulous read, isn't it?" he pressed politely. "Number 5 on the New York Times Best Sellers List for about, say, six months now, I think."

I was secretly impressed by his knowledge but tried my best not to show it.

"I bought it about three years ago and it changed my life practically overnight," the young man revealed, trying his best to make me feel comfortable. "I had been working in London, not getting anywhere with my career, then met and fell in love with a beautiful man who brought me over here…and ah well."

The assistant looked instantly sad, suggesting that things hadn't worked out so well with the relationship…

"The rest is history, as they say."

"Shut up! No way…Me too!" I shouted, struggling to contain my excitement at finding someone else who had the same experience as me. I lowered my voice and whispered, "I used to sneak down behind my makeup counter and hide the book in a drawer, you know…pretend I was counting boxes of mascara but I was really reading chapters of the book. In fact, if it wasn't for this book, I wouldn't be sitting here in this cafe talking to you."

He cracked a knowing smile, then held out his hand and introduced himself, "I'm Jackson."

"I'm Willow."

Look at you girl, meeting perfect strangers in New York! Whatever would Geneviève say!

"May I?" Jackson pointed at the free seat next to mine.

"Please do," I responded, feeling very pleased with myself. I could just picture the girls back at Devonshire's. If only they could see me now.

"It's a long way to come to buy a kettle, is it not?" he pressed gently, while sitting back in his seat, long arms folded across his chest.

"Suppose so. After the night and morning I've had, I was parched. I needed a strong cup of tea. Thought I'd have a root around in this old store y'know, see what I could find…" There was no way I was going to start telling him about my dramatic arrival.

"So, what did you do in the store back home?" he asked, leaning in closer. Scrutinising me in a slightly unsettling manner, reminding me of the brief conversation we had earlier.

"I was a counter manager in the beauty hall. I've been a makeup artist for… let me see…" I made a quick calculation, "8 years."

Jackson's eyes lit up. "Really? You're not by any chance looking for work, are you?"

His line of questioning took me by surprise.

"Will be soon. I was going to take a few weeks to settle in first. You know, buy some curtains, paint the apartment...find my way about town."

Jackson placed his hand down loudly on the table, causing my tea to spill in the saucer.

"Drapes. Darling," he stated in a self-assured manner.

"What?" I asked, wondering what the hell he was going on about now.

"Drapes not curtains, at least that's what they are called over here."

"Oh…I see." My spirits plunged; this conversation was taking far more energy from me than most.

"But don't waste your time," he declared confidently.

"What do you mean?" I asked, feeling slightly confused.

What's he talking about now?

"Job hunting? This is New York, honey. It's all about *who* you know, not *what* you know! If you don't act now, you'll still be searching the classifieds two years from now."

"Oh, I see," I nodded, feeling instantly deflated, I felt my shoulders sink. "Like that is it?"

Jackson leaned across the table, calmly patting my shoulder, "Don't look so worried," he said quietly. "I hold a lot of sway here and I know there's a position they're looking to fill." His blue eyes glinted wickedly under the cafe strip lighting, highlighting his perfect complexion.

I felt my spirits instantly resurge.

"Tell me more!"

That morning, Jackson Dart and I discovered a lot about each other over tea and scones. Not only did we share a love for the craft of applying makeup and books on the 'Law of Attraction,' there seemed to be an undercurrent of something deeper running through our conversation. Something which left me feeling strangely and immediately at ease in his company.

***

With a huge part of me still reeling from last night's revelations about the serious relationship Rick had been involved in for the seven years prior to his leaving for Glasgow, I returned to the apartment. As I put the key in the door lock, I felt a sense of trepidation wash over me.

What will I find this time? I thought to myself as I turned the key in the lock, breath baited with anticipation.

A dead body? I shuddered, as I stepped out of my outdoor shoes and into the white flannel ones by the door which, judging by the gold logo, had more than likely been stolen from a fancy hotel in Asia.

Will she *be here scooping up the last few traces of her expensive lingerie?*

My mind whirred like a Swiss clock on speed, as I conjured up visions of how she might look.

And why did Rick leave her so abruptly? More to the point, why did he pick someone like me over this woman who he had been with for all those years?

Off to the right-hand side of my peripheral vision, I noticed a red flashing light on the telephone answering machine. The anxiety in my stomach intensified.

Could it be her? What would she say? Should I play the message?

The palms of my hands were wet with sweat. I knew there was no-one in the apartment and I also knew that curiosity would get the best of me. I picked up the receiver and pressed play.

"Hi Rick, It's your mom here. I can't wait to hear all about your news. Call me when you get this. Love you."

Breathing a sigh of relief, I surmised from her voice alone, that she would most likely be in her early 60s. Judging by the clipped tones of her New York accent, I could tell she had been very well educated, just like her son. Thinking that Rick must have told his mum about our wedding, I carefully replaced the receiver, eyes darting from side to side as I looked around me, making sure that no-one was watching, which, all told, was a pretty daft thing to do seeing as I was alone and 14 flights up a building in Queens.

I went into the kitchen and unboxed the kettle, making sure to check that the plug was the American version and not the British one as I didn't want to be electrocuted before having my first cup of home-brewed tea. The card from the pest control company lay on the kitchen table, signed by the operator, telling me that the extermination job had been done. I pushed it aside and breathed a sigh of relief, realising for the first time how stressed I had been feeling about the whole incident. Ten minutes later, I sat back on the couch and surveyed my surroundings.

Who would have thought it? Me? Living in bloody New York!!! Well, even if it is Queens, all this place needs is a good clean and a woman's touch. Now, I have my kettle, I can make myself endless cups of tea while cleaning the apartment. I wonder if there is an Ikea nearby.

I took a sip of Earl Grey and let my imagination roam... *some nice bright cushions are just what this place needs, oh and maybe a new silk bedspread and some down pillows...* I thought of how different my life is now to only two months ago prior to that fateful meeting with Rick.

Now, this is the life I deserve. This is the life I have been waiting for. Finally, I've caught a break. The yellow book peeking out of my handbag caught my attention. *Can't wait to see what the next chapter brings!*

What seemed like hours later, I was roused from my snooze on the bed by the sound of a key in the door. Bolting upright and manically wiping the trail of saliva from the side of my mouth, I attempted to figure out where I was, what time of day it was and what country I was in as the familiar sound of Rick's whistling brought me to the here and now.

"Babe? Where are you? It's freezing out!" he said, as he walked into the bedroom, nervously studying me, trying to figure out what kind of mood I was in.

"I know," I replied coldly. "Feels like 5 below."

"So, you ventured out then? All by yourself?" he enquired, as he took off his overcoat, hanging it up in the bedroom wardrobe. His face lit up as his brow arched quizzically. I adored how he made that expression.

"Yes!" I replied, matter-of-factly. "Made it all the way to D'Arcy's all by myself. No one spoke to me. No one tried to rob me at gunpoint and no, I did not interrupt any drug deals."

"Cheeky!" he retorted, flashing a wry smirk, his cold face creasing into a smile.

"Oh! But I did meet a lovely guy from London!" I smacked the blankets on the bed. "Jackson. Jackson Dart. In fact, I might even have got myself a job." I beamed up at Rick, proud of my achievements, wanting him to feel happy for me.

"Wait a minute. Slow down," Rick held up his hands. "D'Arcy's? Jackson? A job?" Rick turned his back on me and walked into the galley kitchen. His gait appeared to stiffen. "You've only been here five minutes…what's the big rush?"

This wasn't the enthusiastic response I had anticipated.

"Oh, don't be so uptight, if I don't act quickly, I'll still be reading the classifieds two years from now!" I repeated what Jackson had said.

"Classifieds?" Rick turned around and stared at me. "Where are you getting this stuff from?" he huffed. "Babe, this is New York not Glasgow, you've got to be careful who you talk to," he winced, causing my spirits to plummet.

"Yeah, right, like I don't know how to take care of myself!" I didn't want to, but I could feel myself starting to pout. "I spoke to *you*, didn't I?"

What is his freakin' problem?

"Ok. Ok," he nodded. "That was different."

He moved in closely, placing his cold hands around my waist. "Just be careful out there, that's all I'm asking." He kissed my ear lobe. I stood unresponsive. Perplexed. Unsure of how to react.

Registering my detachment, Rick fetched two crystal tumblers from the cupboard. Remaining silent, he poured out two whiskies. As he turned around to hand me the glass, I noticed he looked pensive, deep in thought. I had never seen him look this way before.

"Jackson you say?" he asked again.

I stared at my glass.

"You must know by now I don't drink whisky unless it has Irn Bru in it."

My fruitless attempt at humour washed over his head. Rick was deep in thought. In a fog, miles away from me.

"Yes. Jackson," I replied slightly perplexed. "Do you know him?"

"About 6 ft. 3? White? Black hair?" he enquired further, growing antsier by the minute.

"Yeah, that would be him."

"Yes…I know him. Everyone knows Jackson…he's worked on and off with my 'ex' for the past few years. We met at Business School years ago in London."

"Oh…I see. Well, he appeared very nice and friendly to me," I stated matter-of-factly, inwardly annoyed at hearing the words 'my ex.'

But Rick wasn't finished yet.

"There's a ton of department stores in New York, why did you have to apply to D'Arcy's?" The pitch of his voice heightened, "Couldn't you have gone to Macy's or Nordstrom? Why D'Arcy's, for chrissakes?"

His outburst startled me. Speechless, I stared back at him, defiantly but not knowing what to say. I watched on as he removed each shoe and threw it into the corner of the room.

I don't get this. I just don't get it.

Standing up, I cleared my throat.

"You know, I thought for a minute you would have been pleased for me, pleased that I'm trying to get a job and earn some money."

The disappointment in my voice was palpable, "But no! Not you! You go and have a hissy fit. I mean, what's your problem? Most husbands would be delighted that their wives want to go out to work!" There. I had said it. Said what was on my mind. And he could like it or leave it.

Feeling self-righteous that I had asserted myself, I noticed Rick's expression had changed to one of mild shock. I sensed that he realised he had overstepped the mark and tried his best to placate me, but his expression could not hide the fact that he was unhappy with my decision. An inexplicable tension mounted inside me.

I pointed to the red lipstick stained mirror in the adjoining bathroom, "After all, it hasn't exactly been the best start to married life, has it?"

Rick sat on the edge of the bed and held his head in his hands, ruffling his hair as he spoke.

"I'm sorry Willow. None of this has gone to plan." Looking at me, he stood up and swept into the base of my neck, snuggling, kissing me gently as he ran his fingers down my spine. I froze. Once again, I remained unresponsive to his touch as the anxiety roared in the pit of my stomach.

Noticing my frosty demeanour, Rick changed tack, "Look, why don't you go get changed into that slinky black dress I like? You know, the one that sparkles?"

Melting slightly, I gasped as he kissed my earlobe but felt somewhat disappointed in myself that he appeared to be able to win me over so easily.

"And… there's some folks I'd like you to meet."

Finally, I thought. I was starting to think he was ashamed of me.

***

An hour later, Rick and I stole our way down Grand Avenue trying to cadge some heat from wherever we could. Temperatures had plummeted to what felt like 10 below, and yet still there were people out on the street, going about their daily business.

Standing in Paulo's Pizzeria outdoor patio area, my stomach in knots, I pulled Rick in closer, staring in his eyes.

"Will they like me?" I asked, feeling faintly hopeful.

"Like you?" he replied, aghast that I could dare ask such a question." They're gonna love ya!"

"I feel sick. I need a drink."

"C'mon Willow," Rick held me by the arm, stopping me from slipping on an icy patch. "You must have done this countless times before, right?"

"Not really, maybe once or twice at the most, but that was with Finn's parents and I knew they didn't like me from the get-go."

"That scumbag who went out and got someone else pregnant when he was still going out with you?"

"Let's not talk about him. He's in the past," I declared, determined to move on with the conversation.

"Damn right he is," replied Rick. "What kind of guy does something like that?"

Secretly delighted with his internal view of me, I began to relax in the knowledge that maybe this situation would turn out to be easier than I previously thought.

Feeling tipsy from the potent mix of jet lag, nerves and the mix of alcoholic drinks, I could feel the effects of the alcohol almost immediately. Rick noticed it too.

"You're such a cheap date, Willow!" he laughed as he noticed my complexion flush with colour after slipping on the ice for the third time.

"I can't help it," I giggled, hanging on for dear life to his jacket sleeve.

"C'mon, we better get a move on. We don't want to be late." Rick looked at his watch.

"Oops!"

Feeling the sense of trepidation mount in my stomach, I suddenly felt a wave of shyness come over me as my fragile confidence instantly evaporated.

How the hell am I going to handle myself feeling like this?

***

Jake's Restaurant was packed with a well-to-do clientele who all looked like regulars, calling the waiters by their first names. The atmosphere was rowdy in a friendly kind of way, with regulars picking their way through the throng queuing up outside. The décor matched the punters in a strange kind of way: shabby chic nouveau riche is how I would have described it. The scent of money mingled with the aroma of grilled steaks and chateaubriand, while the women displayed every expensive label you could think of on their handbags.

Rick strode on ahead pulling me close behind him as we made our way towards a round table in the centre of the room. I felt consumed with fear at the thought of meeting this new crowd of people. Thankfully a familiar face stood out. It belonged to Jackson, the assistant I had met in D'Arcy's Department Store. One by one, Rick introduced me to his family and friends. His mother, Rosa, wore a classic pink sheath dress adorned with a string of pearls and carried herself in a perfectly straight manner. Her dark hair was styled in a classic bob, similar to my own, while her nails were painted in the exact same shade as her pink lipstick. She appeared well put together in an 'old money' kind of way. Rick's father, also called Ricky, was a force to be reckoned with as he dominated the room, but in a good way. He had charm written all over his face and I instantly realized where Rick got his confidence from. I felt myself ease into the night. Slowly, but surely, I began to relax.

Two merry hours must have passed as the dinner was served accompanied by lashings of champagne, wines and spirits.

They seem like a nice family, I thought as I reveled in the stories being told at the table. Rick's family originally hailed from the Dominican

Republic and had settled in Queens during the early 60's. I could tell they were proud of their son's career in finance. His mother's eyes shone with pride each time he spoke. He was a lucky man to be raised in a family like that.

Towards the end of the evening, Rick put his arm around me and asked for everyone to be quiet.

"Mom, Dad...I'm sorry you never got to our wedding in Scotland, but I've brought you a little memento of the day."

Rick put his hand into the inside pocket of his jacket and pulled out a brown envelope filled with black and white pictures of our wedding day. It was the first time I had seen them.

He passed the pictures around as I gawped in awe at how beautiful we both looked bedecked out in all our finery. Rick wore the traditional Scottish Campbell tartan while I wore an intricate beaded velvet gown. Rosa gasped and appeared tearful. I felt bad for her, missing her only son's wedding,

I thought back to our conversations while planning the wedding and remembered that Rick had told me of the awful relationship he had with his mother and father. Now, seeing them in person, I was confused. This didn't look anything like the dysfunctional relationship he had told me about. In fact, the more I looked at the woman, the sadder I felt for her.

"I'm sorry you weren't able to make it over for our big day, Mrs. Delgado," I offered.

Rosa looked at me with a confused expression as her son shifted uncomfortably in his seat.

"What do you mean?" she asked. "We never got invited!"

Rick cleared his throat and beckoned the waiter over, "Another round please, Charlie."

I stared hard at Rick.

How could you do that to your own mother? I thought. *Not inviting her to*

your wedding?

I made a mental note to question him about it later. Now was not the time. My mood plummeted as doubt once again filled my mind. *Why would he do that?*

"Can I see those photos?"

My attention was immediately drawn by the sound of an Irish lilt emanating from a man who had been standing on the perimeter of the crowd. He appeared to know Rick, as he looked at my husband with a questioning gaze. I wondered who the stranger was.

"What a beautiful bride," he said wistfully, staring at me and then at the photo. There was something about the way he looked at me. It was as if he was staring deep into my soul. He unnerved me.

Rick grabbed the photo out of his hand, "Hey Jake! What about me? Don't I look handsome?" he asked, but everyone had moved on with their conversations. I watched on as the Irish man left in the direction of the bar. Now I knew his name, I wondered who he was.

Just then, a woman appeared at our table. She was about 5ft 8 inches tall and wore her hair in a messed-up pile on the top of her head, adding another couple of inches. Her hour-glass figure caught the attention of both the men and the women in the group.

"Hello Rick," she said. Then she nodded to Mr. and Mrs. Delgado.

Rick looked up from staring at his image in the photograph.

"Isabella!" he gasped, causing me to startle at the mention of her name. *Isabella?* That name struck like a dagger. *Oh my God it's her!* "What the hell are you doing here? I thought I told you to stay away!" he snarled. I had never seen this nasty side of Rick before and it shocked me.

"Don't you dare talk to Isabella like that," said Rick's dad.

She turned her attention to me.

"Who's this?" she asked looking straight through me, chewing gum as she eyed me up and down.

"What are you doing here? I thought I told you to stay away," Rick repeated.

Not quite sure how to respond, I remained silent as Rick put his arm protectively around me, presenting me to the table.

"Bella, this is Willow. My wife.

Silence.

"Excuse me? Did you say 'wife'?" Isabella's eyes narrowed as she spoke.

I swallowed hard. I felt the colour rise in my cheeks. Peering up at Rick's face, the devastation I felt was palpable.

"Didn't you tell her?" I bleated, as confusion and disappointment filled me with despair.

Never in my life had my presence elicited such a reaction from a group of strangers. Rick instinctively knew what was coming as he clutched my shoulders tightly, like he was holding on for dear life.

I couldn't take my eyes off Isabella. I could feel her analysing every aspect of me, from the shoes I wore to the hair follicles on the top of my head, while I, like any other woman in my position, wondered why Rick had chosen me over this exotic looking vision of beauty standing in front of me.

I was shaken from my thoughts as a thick New Jersey drawl spat at me.

"You got married?" Isabella gawped. "To that?"

I shuddered. Cut to the bone by her cruel words, an all-consuming anger bellowed up from deep within me. She had called me 'That,' the expression I most hated from my childhood. The word one particularly nasty set of foster parents had used when they were talking about me to the social worker or when they had chastised me in public. Isabella had referred to me as 'That,' like I was a piece of shit on the bottom of her shoe.

"What did you just say?" I jostled out of Rick's arm, lunging towards her perfectly made up face. As we stared each other out, I heard another voice ringing in my left ear.

"What did she just say?" Isabella looked around. "What kind of freakin' accent is that?"

I continued to stare back at Isabella while Rick's father attempted to placate the crowd. One thing I had learned in foster care was how to take care of myself. Onlookers were enjoying the free spectacle while a slew of waiters rushed around looking mightily miffed at the proceedings.

"Ladies! Ladies! Calm down!" Rick's father pleaded to our better nature, but Isabella's nostrils continued to flare as she took a stiletto heeled step towards Rick and I. Hands on hips, she spat, "So where did you dig her up from?"

"Stop it, Bella!" Rick pointed his finger in Isabella's face, "I'm warning you."

"Don't you dare tell me what to do, Rick Delgado. Not now! Not ever! And certainly not while I'm carrying your baby." Isabella declared, one hand cupping her tiny belly. Everyone stopped what they were doing and looked at Isabella, then at Rick, then at me.

What? No…this can't be happening. Not again!

I turned and slapped Rick hard across the right cheek. "You bastard," I shouted as a sick feeling erupted inside me. I turned away from the crowd and made my way towards the exit.

"Wait! Don't go!" called Rick as he rushed after me. "Hold on Willow."

I turned to face him.

"Give me your keys," I demanded.

Rick had no choice but to hand over his set of keys.

"Really Rick?" I shouted. "This is how you choose to introduce me to your family?"

"But Willow...none of this adds up! It can't be mine..." he wailed, frantically. "I've been with you in Glasgow for the last six weeks...how can that baby be mine?"

Over his shoulder I could see Isabella being escorted away by Rick's mother. I shook my head in disgust and turned and left the scene. Throwing myself into the back seat of a waiting yellow cab. That's when I noticed that Rick did not follow me.

"Manhattan Heights please."

Oh boy, what a sucker I've been.

The Agent Provocateur underwear. The lipsticked message across the bathroom mirror. Now I had seen her for myself, a vast swathe of questions presented themselves. The most pressing of them all was how could Rick have been with someone like that for seven years only to dump her and marry me? Me, who bought utilitarian underwear from Primark and used a lip brush to ensure an expensive lipstick would last a whole year? It just didn't add up.

***

The taxi ride back to the apartment took an eternity. The driver had attempted to chat to me but the expression on my face told him to back off. He turned on the radio as Nilsson belted out 'Everyone's Talking at Me' from Midnight Cowboy. I retreated into myself as I envisaged Isabella and Rick together. I told myself I only had to hold it together for another ten minutes. *You can do it Willow,* I encouraged, *you've done it before, you can do it again. Keep it together. No one needs to see the tears. You can do it.*

On our arrival at the apartment block, I had paid the driver the money and bolted from his taxi before he had had the chance to ask me if I needed change. Catching my reflection in the mirror, it soon struck me why the driver looked so relieved to get me out of his taxi. I looked a right old mess. Blood-shot, puffy eyes, a runny nose and the residue of spilled champagne on my fingers.

As I reached the sanctuary of the apartment, loud sobs exploded out of me as I struggled through the tears to put the key in the keyhole. At last, I had got in, hauled my coat off, accidentally banged my knuckles off the door handle, kicked my shoes off and thrown myself on top of the unmade bed. I lay there sobbing into my pillow, while trails of black mascara made train tracks on the 300-count white bed linen. I couldn't have cared less that I was potentially ruining his expensive bed linens. At that moment in time, laundry was the least of my worries.

Thirty minutes later, the sound of loud knocking at the door shook me from my thoughts.

Go away!

But the knocking persisted. I could hear Rick call my name. While my gut instinct told me to stay put on top of the bed, I remembered I had taken his door key. I stood up and walked towards the entrance of the apartment.

Ever so slowly, I opened the door, while trying my best to stop the tears from falling.

"Willow. Look, I'm sorry. It's not what you think." Rick wore a hang-dog expression, as raindrops ran off his overcoat.

"Go Away!" I shouted, hardly able to even look at him. "Just get away from me!"

"You gotta believe me!" Rick pleaded. "She's nuts! She wasn't supposed to be there."

Seething with the well of anger that was swirling inside me, I found the strength from within to grab Rick by the arms and turn him around, pushing him towards the door. Three months of intense ballet barre classes had made me stronger than I realised.

"Willow, please, listen to me..."

Opening the door, I stood by it, indicating for Rick to leave. "Out," I pointed.

Rick went to say something, then thought better of it. Staring at the floor, he exited his own apartment. I slammed the door shut then leaned against it, staring at the apartment interior before me. As if seeing it clearly for the first time. Slowly, I exhaled and slid my back down the door, falling to a heap on the polished wooden floorboards. A wail of sadness erupted from within as I lay in the fetal position on the floor.

That night, the New York skyline twinkled like diamonds in the dust, peeking through the slim gaps in the blinds that weren't shut quite tightly. The dusky interior took on a magical light. From my position on the floor, I noticed the phone blinking furiously away. Bereft, I briefly thought about phoning Geneviève back in Glasgow but the shivers running down my spine informed me that was a very bad decision. I resolutely decided against it. What a field day she would have with this!

Tonight, I would face being alone in New York. Eventually I gathered myself together and like any other adult in my position, I sought solace in the kitchen where I poured myself a large goblet of comforting red Syrah wine, cranked up the heat, pulled on my warmest fleece pj's and threw myself, once more, on top of the gigantic king size bed.

Rick is the father of Isabella's baby; the thought would not leave me.

4

PREP AND GO!

Awakening with a jolt, it took me a few moments to register my surroundings. The previous night had been rough, and the sheets on Rick's bed bore all the hallmarks of a fractious night spent tossing and turning. I had curled myself up into a ball in a bid to keep warm and had gathered the pillows around me into a protective shield, forming a makeshift wall in a vain attempt to keep the outside world as far away as possible.

Rubbing the sleep out of my eyes, I stepped onto the cold floor, trembling slightly as the sensation shot through me, and made my way towards the window. That morning I saw New York through the curtain of a blizzard, huge pillow-like snowflakes falling silently from far above me. My heart pounded as I watched one little snowflake spinning around as it made its way down to the street below. It would reach its destination in only a few short seconds and with a sudden 'splat!' it would all be over.

That's when it dawned on me that I had an interview to get ready for - my interview at D'Arcy's. The interview that Rick did not want me to go for.

I had never been more determined to secure a job than I was at that moment.

As there is no better way to start the day than with a mug of steaming hot tea, I made my way to the kitchen and switched on my brand-new kettle. Waiting patiently in the freezing kitchen for the kettle to boil, I turned the thermostat way up as I attempted to keep myself warm by dancing ridiculously to The Waitresses belting out 'Christmas Wrapping.' Then it struck me.

Wait! It's only 5 weeks till Christmas!

Kettle boiled, I steeped the tea bag for a few seconds before grabbing my mug of tea and the yellow book I had left balancing precariously on the arm rest of the sofa the day before. I made my way back to Rick's bedroom, taking care to avert my eyes from the last vestiges of red lipstick on the bathroom mirror.

Five minutes later, snuggling under the warmth of the feather duvet, I lay back against the pillow, took a sip of tea and exhaled as I surveyed my surroundings. I decided then to open the yellow book at a random page.

'Harmonise the mind by seeking strength in solitude.'

Wow! Bloody spot on again!

I had never felt more alone than I did at that moment but sensing that I was somehow supposed to be in this place at this exact time, I felt a wave of calmness wash over me.

As my gaze settled on the view from the bedroom window, I decided to get up, have a shower, get dressed and then head down to the streets below to find a new outfit to wear to my interview. Just for once, today was going to be all about me. Catching sight of the bathroom mirror, I made a mental note to buy a bottle of Windex.

Later that morning as I stepped out onto the sidewalk, I noticed the snowflakes had stopped falling and instead, the sun shone brightly, the clouds clearing away to reveal a sparkling navy-blue sky. The biting cold air swirled around my ankles, chilling me to the bone. I had to give it to Rick, he was right about New York winters, and they made our Scottish ones seem like springtime in comparison.

My interview was scheduled for 2:00pm leaving me plenty of time to buy a new black outfit. Remembering the makeup artists, I had already seen in action at D'Arcy's, it was obvious that a high standard of appearance was expected if I were to succeed at getting the job.

Further down the street, I noticed a tiny boutique named *Cupcake*. The window display showed an array of exotic lingerie, but I could see that they also stocked a range of classically designed separates, just the thing for interview attire.

One hour later, I had chosen a chic black boat-neck cashmere top and a pair of smartly tailored cigarette pants all charged to Rick's credit card.

Serves him right.

I felt a wave of excitement as I watched the sales assistant delicately pack up my purchases, placing the garments carefully in a pristine white carrier bag embossed with the store's name. Now, all that remained was to find some glass cleaner.

Back in Rick's apartment, I broke the silence of being alone and turned on the radio once more. I carefully laid everything out on top of the bed, making sure not to crease the cashmere, as Dionne Warwick sang, "I say a little prayer for you." Next, I unpacked my stiletto shoes, normally reserved for nights out where little walking was required. These would do for the moment as I figured that if I were lucky enough to secure a job at D'Arcy's, the heels would soon be replaced by my trusty Repetto ballet flats, a staple of my work wardrobe. But first, I had a little job to attend to.

I turned the volume up to as high as my hearing could stand and danced to Sister Sledge sing the lyrics to 'Thinking of You.' The song always raised my spirits. Stepping back from the mirror, I decided that now would be the best time to bring out the cleaning supplies I had purchased from a quaint dollar store two blocks away. On went the black rubber elbow-length washing up gloves complete with shocking pink feathers, and the ubiquitous bottle of Windex. Rubbing with all my might, the significance of erasing Isabella's artwork from Rick's bathroom mirror was not lost on me.

Housework done; I smoothed my hair into a shiny, glossy bob before applying a slick of Dolce Vita by Dior - Isabella wasn't the only woman in this city with a passion for iconic red lipstick.

Later that afternoon, for the second time that day, I strode out of Manhattan Heights, hoping against all hope that I would return as a gainfully employed resident of Queens, New York.

After last night…it's the least I deserve.

5

SHARKS ON THE SHOP FLOOR

"Paperwork? What do you have for me?"

Gigi Gerson sat across from me, perched elegantly on her transparent Starck Empire chair, nails immaculate, painted in a soft ballet pink which perfectly matched her lipstick. The white walls of her office were stylishly offset by her massive white Formica desk, which in turn was accented by a single white vase containing white tulips.

Bit of a theme going on here, I thought as I surveyed my surroundings.

"I have a temporary work visa," I replied, making my best attempt at trying to sound full of confidence. "I'm expecting my Green Card any day now."

This was a downright lie, Rick and I both knew that realistically, we would be waiting a year plus for the green card to come in. Scared to look up at her, I continued, "They tell me it can take a while." Then I stared at my feet once more. Hopeful.

Shit! What the hell do I know about any of this stuff? Jeez, Willow, keep it together!

Mrs. Gerson, known to her employees as Mrs. G, stared back at me with an all-knowing look, her chiseled cheekbones expertly highlighted with a sweep of honey blush. On the surface she was attractive in a well lived, handsome kind of way. I could tell she was most likely nearing the end of her 50s, the lines around her artificially plumped lips a dead giveaway. Then again, she could be a smoker. Her svelte figure had been well looked after and if her office was anything to go by, then I was sure she held a membership at the prestigious gym, just a block away. I got the distinct impression she was a force to be reckoned with.

"This all seems to be in order," Mrs. G stared hard at me. "Can you start today? I have a vacancy I need to fill urgently."

What? I wasn't expecting that!

Dismayed, I smiled broadly, stood up and offered my hand in agreement. I saw Mrs. G's eyes dart quickly to the bottle of hand sanitizer on her desk as she made a split-second decision whether or not to shake my hand.

Charming…

But thinking better of it, my new boss took my hand and shook it vigorously.

"Thanks, Mrs. Gerson. I won't let you down." *Smile Willow, keep smiling.*

Mrs. G motioned for me to walk with her towards her office door. Once again, I saw her eyes dart from the door handle to the bottle of hand sanitizer.

"I'm sure you won't," she sighed, almost as if she had said this sentence a thousand times before.

Opening the door to let me out, we were both taken by surprise when a tall young man fell inwards towards us.

"Jackson! Quelle Surprise!" Mrs. G flashed a wicked smile in my direction, silently apologising for his behaviour. "I want you to take Willow over to Dior."

I looked over at Jackson and noticed his expression had changed.

"Wouldn't it be better if she worked by me? I mean, just until she finds her feet. You know Dior's not the easiest counter to start on."

Mrs. G's silence coupled with a steely expression made Jackson think twice about his suggestion.

The pinging orchestra of nerves in my belly erupted as I expertly read the situation. I had worked in the industry far too long to be considered naïve, I braced myself for what was to come next just as Jackson interrupted my thoughts.

"Ok Miss Hot Shot! Come with me," Jackson strode ahead of me, expecting me to follow on.

Safely out of earshot from Mrs. G, Jackson bent down a touch and whispered in my ear, "You, my dear, are about to meet the scariest shark on the shop floor. Her last assistant only lasted half a shift."

"Oh, like that is it?" I enquired.

Shit! This is all I freakin' need.

Jackson swaggered through the swing doors with me by his side. I was immediately gripped by that familiar feeling of anxiety and trepidation. No one likes being the new girl, yet here I was, thousands of miles away from home and about to step into my new role as a D'Arcy's Makeup Artist on the Dior counter. I sensed that Jackson felt something too. Was it a sense of pride at having helped me secure the role? Or maybe the feeling of British bravado that one feels when working abroad? Whatever it was, he seemed delighted that he now had a Scottish counterpart to aid and abet him whenever required.

As I marched through the beauty hall, dressed sleekly in black and looking every inch a typical D'Arcy's employee, I noticed Jackson nod and smile at his colleagues. *Quite the popular chap,* I thought as I smiled in tandem with him.

"Here we are!" he announced as we stopped in front of one of the most prestigious counters on the shop floor – all glass and gold and glittering bottles of perfume sparkling like precious jewels under the store lights.

But surprisingly, for a store of this size and stature, there was no one around to greet us.

How strange.

As if reading my thoughts, Jackson piped up, "Bloody typical! Probably out back having a sly fag!"

Just then, a strangely recognisable figure, dressed in a figure-hugging black jersey dress, emerged from the staff entrance onto the shop floor. I stared at the woman but couldn't quite place her. But I didn't need to wait too long. The woman cupped her tiny baby bump as she stared straight through me.

"You!" she shouted in horror.

The familiarity of her New Jersey voice struck me as a wave of despondency ran rough shod over me. "It's you!" I heard myself say, equally horrified, as I took a step back.

Jackson braced himself as his eyes darted from me to Isabella.

Isabella hadn't changed much from the previous night. She still wore her hair high and messily coiffed, like she had just rolled straight out of bed. The shop floor lights glinted off the same bronze barrette, she wore last night.

Manky cow, hasn't even bothered to wash her hair, probably stinks of fag and coffee breath too.

As I stood there looking at her, it was as if all the pieces of a highly confusing jigsaw puzzle were being pieced together at lightning speed. *So, she's the reason Rick didn't want me interviewing here!*

I wanted to get away from her, be out of there. The pinging in my belly intensified at an alarming rate. Like an animal in a life-threatening situation, I chose flight over fight and made my way quickly towards the door that Isabella had just come out of. I could hear Jackson in the foreground shouting, "Willow! Come back! You can't leave now...you only just got here!"

Jackson caught up with me as I made my way to what I now realized was the staffroom locker. Grabbing me by the arm, he hissed in my ear, "What the hell are you playing at?" his eyes bulging maniacally as he attempted to suss me out.

"Why didn't you tell me she worked in here?" I breathed heavily, staring at Jackson, "Or is this all a game to you?" I snarled, losing my rag with the man who had helped me secure a job.

"Look, I thought Mrs. G was going to put you on my counter. I didn't for one-minute think she would put you with her." Jackson looked sheepish, like he had fucked up in a big way. I felt momentarily sorry for him.

"Don't worry about it. You weren't to know. It's not your fault," I emphasized but it all seemed like too little too late.

"I'm sorry Willow," Jackson said.

***

Unbeknownst to both of us, Mrs. G had been watching proceedings on the shop floor and had followed us both to the staffroom.

"Jackson," she called. "I thought I asked you to take Willow to Dior?"

Jackson stood to attention, standing in front of me, shielding me from my new boss' steely stare.

Shit! I thought as I stared at my shoes.

"Oh, Willow just needed a little pep talk from me on how to deal with New Yorkers. You know they can come across as a bit intimidating to us more reserved Brits." I felt Jackson gently pinch the back of my arm as he spoke.

Impressed with his quick thinking I reciprocated pinching his arm, in acknowledgement, as I continued staring at my feet, not daring to look up and catch Mrs. G's gaze.

"Then move along people! What are you waiting for? Get back to work," she demanded, snapping her fingers in a flourish.

There was no choice but to return to the shop floor and face Isabella De La Souza.

***

I had to hand it to Isabella. She behaved as if nothing fazed her as she requested my resume, scanning it intently. A true professional, I would say. I had already anticipated that she would look for some kind of excuse not to have me on the counter, but no matter how hard she looked, that piece of paper was as clean as a whistle.

Across from our station on the shop floor, Jackson took up residence on the Luella Bee Apothecary counter, an organic skincare homage to the honeybee. Just as the bee population was in decline it appeared that so too was Jackson's counter.

As Isabella and I went about our day, she in scornful silence, I in utter trepidation, Jackson watched on intently—he couldn't keep his eyes off both of us, observing our every move as we danced expertly behind the counter, ignoring each other while serving our clients. I was well versed in situations like this and by the looks of things, so too was Isabella.

By mid-afternoon, as the onslaught of lunchtime shoppers began to trickle off, I noticed Mrs. G make her way toward my counter, only to be side-tracked by Jackson staring off into the distance.

"Don't stand around all day gawping, there's a white glove inspection at 3:00pm and you'd better not fail it," she rasped, raising one perfectly groomed eyebrow as she spoke. Jackson stood to attention while attempting to suppress a smirk.

Wow! He's brave!

Despite the trying circumstances of the first day on my new counter, the afternoon seemed to pass quickly. I knew that Isabella and I would each have loved to ask the other a bucketful of questions, but I also knew that neither of us would. Instead, I chose to stand quietly by and observe. Thinking of my colleagues back in Glasgow, I knew that Greta and Co. would have a field day if they knew I was here working alongside my husband's ex.

Ex-Partner? That's when it really hit me. *Was she really his ex or did these two still have something going on that I didn't know about?*

As if on cue, Jackson appeared at my side, "Penny for them?"

Ignoring him, I set about windexing the counter and shelves, making sure to remove the collection of expensive fragrance bottles one by one, safeguarding them as I went.

"Be careful not to daydream on the shop floor, if Mrs. G catches you, you'll know all about it," Jackson declared, hoping to give me the low-down, but his timing was all wrong.

"It's just such a lot to take in, you know?" I replied, my head all over the place. Jackson looked at me like he understood. "And she's so damn beautiful, I mean what the hell does Rick see in me?"

"He sees what I see." Jackson put his arm around me, "Now, c'mon! Snap out of it! Let's go for tea. This place has died a death," he paused, "and Bella is due back any minute."

"Shouldn't we wait till she gets here first? I mean, I don't want to get into trouble on my first day."

"Trouble? I think you've already made a lasting impression, don't you?"

"I suppose so," I replied meekly, as I pondered the day's events, not wanting to dwell too deeply on what had just transpired.

Jackson attempted to cheer me up, "C'mon let's go!" He pulled my arm. "Next time we're on shift together, I'll take you to the Scottish store. They sell Irn Bru and pineapple cakes in there."

What a lovely man! I had only known him five minutes, but it somehow felt like we had known each other for ever. Relaxing in his company, I sensed a smile reverberate across my face.

Despite all the drama, something told me I was going to enjoy working in D'Arcy's and I was determined that no one, including Bella, was going to steal my thunder. Of that at least, I was sure.

6

SCAR TISSUE

Later that evening, I unlocked Rick's apartment door. A heady scent of fresh peonies, combined with a top note of cheap, toxic lemon cleaner, lambasted me, infiltrating my nostrils, leaving a distinctive odour permeating throughout the tiny apartment. Someone had come in while I was gone, and I could only assume it had been Rick. I was right. He had left a tiny white envelope inscribed with the words, *'Let's start afresh? Call me.'*

I placed the card back in its envelope and decided there and then that no, I wouldn't call him. I wasn't going to be won over that easily. I went into the galley kitchen, switched on the kettle before happening upon a blue plastic basin in the bathroom cupboard.

So, Isabella gets sore feet too!

I filled the basin with warm water. I had already noticed an expensive looking jar of lavender bath crystals in the cabinet and surmising that they must belong to Isabella, I poured a generous amount under the running water. If I had bought them, I would only have used a capful. Isabella hadn't struck me as the organic-hippy-chick kind of girl, but perhaps even she suffered from stress occasionally?

My feet throbbed. Eight hours of standing in three-inch heels had taken its toll. Now, the only activity I wished to pursue was changing out of my stilettos and soaking my feet in the basin of warm lilac water.

Today had been a psychological head-bender and I wanted it over with. As I sat in front of the TV, with a mug of steaming hot tea in hand, a faint memory from decades ago crept into my thoughts.

You can only do your best. The world loves a trier.

Two fat tears splodged onto my cheeks in quick succession. *If Mum and Dad had still been alive, they would have told me what to do…*

***

That next morning, I awoke, got dressed and stood to attention in front of the bedroom closet mirror. The nervous orchestra in my stomach pinged on cue as I envisioned the day ahead. It was only 08:45 am but I had already decided to splurge and take a cab to work just to negate any chance of me turning up late. I didn't want to give Isabella any opportunity to chastise me.

At 09:45 am, as I entered the hallowed halls of D'Arcy's Department Store, I summoned up the courage to walk alone onto the shop floor. As if on cue, the elastic bands pinged in the pit of my belly as I tried to say "Hello" to a few of my 'colleagues' who I recognised had been on duty the day before, then headed straight for Dior. Straight ahead, I could see her standing there, waiting on me…ready to pounce.

"Sit down," Isabella demanded.

"Good morning to you too!" I replied, staring back at her carefully made up face while refusing to look at the black leather chair.

I wonder what time she got out of bed to achieve that.

"I said sit!" Isabella snapped, looking at me with that same bitch-slapped expression I had seen in the restaurant that terrible evening.

"Why?" I asked, refusing to back down as every inch of me prepared to do battle, as a freezing chill snaked down my spine causing me to shiver slightly.

"You're a mess! That's why!" Isabella scanned me from top to toe, cruelly lingering on the scar on my right cheek, a leftover reminder of a basal cell removal from years ago.

"Charming," I replied, knowing full well I had taken over an hour to get ready that morning, leaving absolutely nothing to chance. Still, here she was trying her best to trip me up.

Full of trepidation, I concluded it was probably best, in this instance, to do as she told me. I sat down in the chair reserved for clients, making sure not to break eye contact with her. Years ago, my dad had told me never to lose eye contact with a dog that was threatening to bite, and now I found myself putting his advice to good use in a New York City beauty hall. The thought of it made me smirk.

"What's so funny?" she asked, staring through me.

"Oh…nothing!" I chirped, clasping my hands tightly as I settled into the chair, wiggling my bum into a more comfortable position, knowing that by doing so, I was pissing her off even more in the process.

Isabella grabbed the selection of brushes that she had left out to dry overnight, I noticed then that a few of my new co-workers had gathered around to watch. In unison, I guessed that none of us could believe that I was going to allow Isabella to get to work on my face.

OK! Here goes nothing! God help me!

"Where do I begin?" Isabella sighed as she scrutinized every line and wrinkle on my face. "I got my work cut out!" I looked up at her briefly only to be reviled by the look of disgust on her face. I settled my gaze on the backs of my hands which were now clasped tightly in my lap.

The next ten minutes passed uncomfortably as Isabella worked heavy-handedly, making sure to focus in on the scar tissue on my right cheek.

"Do you have to be so rough?" I called out angrily as she tore at my skin with the concealer brush. "Do you treat all your clients like this?"

"Only those that need it," she spat.

Heartless bitch!

"This is all about Rick, isn't it?" I asked, one eyebrow arched in defiance as I dared stare up at her.

Isabella stopped what she was doing and stared down at me, looking at me, as if seeing me properly for the first time.

"Rick?" she snarled. "He's the father of my child. Don't you forget it."

"Is he?" I glared, defying her to answer me.

My question cut through her like a knife as she stopped the makeover.

"Do it yourself," she threw the foundation brush at me.

"Isabella! That's enough now," a man scolded.

I looked up to see Jake, the Irishman who had been in the restaurant on the night that Rick had introduced me to his family.

"You never mind her," he winked. "She's a fiery one," he chirped as he vacuumed around the counter.

As Isabella exited the shop floor, Jackson appeared at my side.

"My God! What happened? What did you say? I've never seen Bella look so upset!"

Part of me felt bad for Isabella.

"Nothing to worry about," I shrugged as I smiled at Jake.

But I *was* worried. Isabella apparently still has feelings for my husband.

Have I come all this way to swap one work hell for another? This unsettling thought lingered with me for the rest of the morning.

7

TRANSFORMATION

The remainder of the shift passed smoothly as I became acquainted with my new colleagues and customers. Lisa from Perfumery stood opposite me, helping me with some of the finer details of a D'Arcy's counter. Little did she know that, location aside, D'Arcy's was just like every other department store I had worked in. The only difference was that at D'Arcy's, the diverse clientele seemed to know exactly what they wanted and weren't shy at asking for it.

Half an hour into my morning shift, it soon became obvious to me that I was being watched closely from all quarters. I already sensed Isabella intently observing my every move as I slowly got to grips with the inner running of the store, making me feel like a caterpillar caught under a microscope. But the one person who unnerved me the most was Mrs. G. Every so often, I would catch her watching me as I looked up from performing a makeover, but when we locked eyes, she would hold her gaze, causing me to look away. Occasionally, she would bring over new clients and introduce me to them as her "Brit Girl." She appeared to take some pride in my national identity as she jokingly told her clients that she had hired me to stop Jackson— "her other Brit employee"—from feeling so lonely. I secretly hoped that this hadn't been the only reason she had hired me.

Shortly after lunch, I noticed a hefty woman appear in front of Jackson's counter.

"Jackson! Look at what you did to me!" an unmistakable Jamaican lilt echoed around the beauty hall as the woman pointed at a patch of angry crusted pimples on her face.

"You should never have sold me that toner!" she cried. "It's toilet cleaner!"

Jackson breathed out heavily, making his annoyance known. No matter whether you worked in New York, London or Paris, nobody appreciated having their brand's products bitch slapped in front of a full house of customers.

Inhaling impatiently, Jackson stared at the woman, "I thought I told you to use it sparingly? I told you to use just a little!"

I sensed the tension building as the Jamaican woman shifted her weight impatiently from foot to foot, looking like she was ready to do battle. "You never told me that!" she bellowed, as the other shoppers came to a halt, looking around to see where the commotion was coming from.

Oh no! This is not going to be good.

I knew that Jackson had already taken a verbal assault from Mrs. G earlier in the shift about the state of his counter, and now I could see her walking towards him, eyebrows arched in anticipation, ready once again to do battle with her "Brit boy" cohort.

It was now or never. I stepped away from my counter and took up position in front of Jackson's client.

"Why don't I have a look?"

The Jamaican woman, Ms. Sondra, peered down at me, staring hard as she tried in vain to place my accent.

"You need some chamomile on that to calm it down," I suggested. "Hold on I've got just the thing." Delving into Luella Bee's Apothecary cabinets, I rummaged around in search of some cotton pads and a bottle of chamomile lotion. As I walked back towards Ms. Sondra, I realised that it was not going to be as easy to pacify her as

I had first thought.

"Wow! Hold on there, missy!" Ms. Sondra stopped me. "You're not putting any more garbage on my face! I'm sick of you people always trying to sell me stuff and none of it works." In any other situation, Ms. Sondra's gaze would have unnerved me, but I was experienced in conflict deflection. Years of living with Geneviève had taught me that skill.

Seizing the opportunity to walk away, Jackson scampered off the shop floor, leaving me alone to face both Mrs. G and the irate customer.

Nice one. Thank you, Jackson.

I ignored the scathing comments from Ms. Sondra as I gently dabbed at her face with the lotion. Gradually, I felt her begin to relax. I didn't speak. Instead, I allowed her to vent until she ran out of steam. Mrs. G watched in silence as I calmed the situation and Ms. Sondra's complexion. As I slowly got the situation under control, I sensed I was beginning to win over Jackson's customer. After some time, I felt the woman's defenses deflate.

"Can I ask you something?' Ms. Sondra peered inquisitively into my face.

"Go on," I encouraged, not sure what was going to come out of her mouth.

"Do you like what you see when you look in the mirror?" she enquired, staring hard at me.

I realised immediately what she was referring to. Ever since Isabella's early morning attempt at a makeover, my scar tissue had felt as if it was pulsating under my makeup. I felt a sudden wave of self-consciousness sweep over me.

"No. Not always. But I try not to let it get me down. Sometimes I disguise it and sometimes I let it show. Just depends on how I feel."

"I like you!" Ms. Sondra dived in for a hug, unnerving me, shaking me off my firm footing.

"You're such a cutie!" she kept hugging on, "And such a dope accent too! Give me two bottles of that stuff…and you can tell Jackson he can go…never mind, I'll tell him myself!" Ms. Sondra cackled wickedly as she winked at me.

Mrs. G and I watched on as she left the building. I looked at my watch.

"Time for my tea," I said to no one in particular. As I walked by Jackson's counter, I stifled a laugh as I caught him peering up from behind the cash register.

"It's OK. You can get up now. She's gone."

Jackson bowed apologetically as I passed. I had saved his skin, now he owed me one.

After my lunch, dining alone in the store restaurant, I ventured back to my counter. There was no sign of Isabella. *Must be off on one of her vaping breaks.* There were some days when I wished that I had a 20-a-day habit, but no matter how hard I tried I could never bring myself to smoke. The beauty hall floor was quiet, almost completely devoid of customers. I looked at my watch. There was always a dip in the afternoons when the workers returned to their offices and the school run was yet to begin. This was the time of day that I usually dedicated to paperwork and stocking up on supplies in anticipation of the handover to the evening part-timer. Isabella and Jackson were nowhere to be seen and the perfume ladies appeared to be deep in conversation about the previous night's episode of "Housewives of New York City."

I surveyed the floor, hoping to make a few late afternoon sales so that I could reach my target for the day and keep Isabella off my back. To my right, I saw a young woman in her early 20s. Doe-eyed, and endowed with crystal clear green eyes, she had fine, sculpted features and an elegant silk scarf tied bandana-like at the nape of her neck. Her gait told me she was either shy, nervous, or both. I would need to proceed with caution. Years behind the makeup counter had turned me into a bit of a body language expert and in most cases, I had been proven correct.

"Hello," I began approaching her. "Can I help you?" I asked quietly, not quite sure whether I should just leave her alone.

The young woman held up her hand, indicating that she didn't want me to approach. I backed off and buried my head in a mountain of paperwork. Someone else would come along soon, they always did.

Twenty minutes passed, yet still, the young woman stood at the side of my counter, appearing to examine the products, one by one, slowly placing them back on their respective shelves.

What is going on with this woman? She should buy or go away instead of hanging about my counter all day!

Placing my pen down on the paperwork, I decided to approach once more. This time, a little more directly. My stomach was rumbling and the blister on my right heel was starting to complain.

"I'm between clients and have a spare 20 minutes if you'd like to try on some products?" I enquired gently, not wanting to appear too pushy.

The young woman stared straight back at me. Momentarily taken aback, I gulped, hoping not to show my surprise.

"Could you give me some brows and some lashes?"

"Of course. Take a seat." I replied, immediately warming towards the young woman. "My name is Willow. What's yours?" I enquired as I gathered my tools: a pot of powder and eyebrow brush for the brows and a set of false lashes to frame her searing green eyes, as opalescent as the ocean.

"Claudia."

She relaxed a little as she settled into the makeover chair, I felt her trust in me begin to grow. It was then I realised that she had been watching me this whole time, slowly gathering the confidence to ask me to help her. I felt honoured.

Ten minutes later, and with no resistance from my new customer, I decided to push the boat out and applied two delicate flicks of sexy black liquid eyeliner. The results were astonishing as Claudia transformed in front of my eyes.

"Can I see?" she enquired, almost childlike.

Peering intently at her reflection in the mirror, I sensed immediately her self-esteem begin to soar. It was the best part of my job. The side of the job that only other makeup artists know about; the side that builds and accomplishes self-esteem with one deft flick of a brush or eyeliner pen. I smiled back at her.

"Gorgeous!" I exclaimed. "Just gorgeous!"

Getting up off the chair, Claudia grabbed the hand-held mirror out of my hand, looked at me, and then returned her gaze to the mirror.

"Oh my God, you made me look …normal!" she gasped, then returned to stare at her reflection in the mirror once more.

"Yes. You look beautiful," I replied. My heart swelled like it might burst with pride.

Claudia swung around and hugged me tightly, squeezing the very breath out of me. I wondered how long she had been feeling so low.

"Happy?" I asked, tears of joy threatening to spill over onto my cheeks. It wasn't often my job reduced me to tears but today was an exception.

"That's an understatement! Book me in for next week. I got a date with my husband and I want to look like this when he takes me out. Our first wedding anniversary is coming up!" She peered again at her reflection, letting me see behind her emotional guard for just a second, "It's been a tough year."

"I bet it has," I responded while checking the appointment book, "3pm OK for you?"

"Perfect."

Gathering her things, Claudia made her way proudly through the myriad of counters, her bald head gleaming under the bright store lights. Her spirit dazzling other would-be customers who stood aside to let her pass. I turned around to pack away my brushes, noticing at once that the silk headscarf was lying on my counter.

"Claudia! You forgot this!" I shouted, holding up her scarf, waving it in the air as I attempted to grab her attention.

"Don't need it," she hollered back, making her way out of the store. I looked on wistfully, secretly wondering what it must feel like to be excited to go on a date with a loving husband. Feeling forlorn, I returned to my paperwork as Mrs. G walked towards me.

"Willow, come and see me in my office at the end of your shift."

Shit! What have I done?

'Will do! Mrs. G," I replied, attempting to look confident while wiping my sweaty palms with a tissue.

The end of my shift posed a problem. I knew I would now have to think about what to do about the "Rick situation," plus I had to go and see Mrs. G in her office. I waited patiently at the staff entrance, huddled in the doorway as Jackson took an intense drag on a Marlboro. I peered up at him, wondering why he looked so stressed out.

Just then, as if on cue, Isabella exited the building, knocking me off my footing as she barreled by, forcing me to step down onto the pavement.

"Hey!" I called, "Watch where you're going."

Jackson joined in, stubbing out his cigarette under his black leather winkle pickers, "Bella! Wait up!"

Isabella ignored both of us, throwing her head back, bedraggled hair straggling down her long narrow back as she marched down the street at an impressive pace in her three-inch heels. Jackson shrugged his shoulders, peering down at me from his 6-foot 3-inch height.

"C'mon. I'll buy ***you*** a drink. It's about time you got to see how we live it up in Queens!"

I smiled.

Finally! Thought you would never ask!

"OK. But give me five minutes...Mrs. G wants to see me in her office."

I felt as if I had been waiting forever for someone to show me the inside workings of this town but yet, no one had thought of asking me to tag along with them.

Ten minutes later, Jackson led me into Lola's and invited me to sit at the bar. For a moment, it seemed as though I was the only woman amongst this throng of gorgeous, toned, trim men. Jackson stood taller than most, brooding above everyone else at the bar. As he ordered two Singapore Slingers from the bartender, I noticed for the first time how his exquisitely toned arms didn't bulge out like so many of the other men, his physique was different – modest and athletic, lending him an air of poise coupled with a dash of elegance.

Jackson waited patiently as the only other female (besides me) prepared our drinks. Nodding over at me, he motioned for me to sit on the barstool before placing my drink in front of me.

Holding his glass up high in the air, he nodded at me as his face burst into a huge smile, "Willow Campbell-Delgado, it's a pleasure to finally meet you."

I raised my glass to his, "Jackson Dart, it's lovely to meet you too!"

"Cheers!" we said in unison.

"But wait a wee minute…what do you mean by *finally*?" I asked.

"Finally, a true friend," he exhaled as a look of relief seemed to wash over him. "I feel like I've been waiting forever for someone like you to come along."

The intensity of his revelation unnerved me.

"But I don't get it…I'd thought you'd have tons of pals to hang around with," I blurted, mystified, wondering how this gorgeous man could have so few friends.

Jackson peered down at me, his expression changing slightly to one of sadness, "Acquaintances more like. It's so difficult to find real friends in this city. People move around at such a fast pace. I always feel like I'm being left behind."

I felt honoured that he would take me into his confidence so quickly.

"I used to feel like that in Glasgow," I responded, as I remembered how many of my colleagues only stayed for a short while before heading off to pastures new. "But now I am here to stay, so you don't need to worry about me, OK?" I declared with absolute certainty.

Jackson looked away shyly, took a swig of his drink, then turned to face me once more.

"So, tell me about Bella," he asked, one eyebrow arched skyward, "Does she bite?"

"No!" I laughed, "But I fully expect that if she could, she damn well would!"

Jackson took a long, slow drag on his cigarette, inhaling deeply before responding, "Sounds just like our Bella."

Moments passed in silence with no further conversation between us. Jackson appeared to be deep in thought, staring at the dregs of liquid in his glass. Neither of us seemed willing or able to discuss Bella any further. As the awkward silence developed, I decided to break it.

"Earth to Jackson?"

Jackson placed his empty glass on the counter and turned to give me his full attention.

"Sorry. Been a tough day. Mrs. G's been putting the pressure on again," he gulped, tapping his fingers off the table, looking at once vulnerable and out of character.

"Why? What's going on?" I enquired.

Jackson appeared to take a moment or two before deciding whether to divulge any more. Searching my eyes for an indication that he could trust me, before making his big reveal, "I've got a dying counter."

"Oh. I see," I said softly.

Shit. This is awkward. This is all I need. The guy gets me a job and now he could be out on a limb.

I shifted nervously in my chair, trying to find the perfect balance between composed and concerned while attempting not to look too worried for him. I knew he had been having trouble with Mrs. G, but I hadn't thought it was this serious.

"They put me on it as a last-ditch attempt to save it, but it's not working. Don't know what's going to happen next." Looking relieved that he had finally confided in someone, I tried my best to comfort him, but I couldn't think of anything to say. What could I say? I had only just walked in the door and had been invited in by the very guy who was now in trouble.

"Anyway!" he brightened, "'Nuff about me! How are you going to survive working beside the "shark"?"

"You mean Isabella?"

Jackson nodded.

"Don't know," I replied, somewhat unnerved that he had turned the conversation so expertly back to me, "I'll have to figure it out somehow. I've met her kind before, but this is different…way different."

Gulping the last remaining dregs from the bottom of my glass, I found myself overcome with emotion. Perhaps it was the effects of the alcohol, but this offloading of our concerns was catching. Now, it was my turn to divulge.

"I'm a mess!" I blurted.

Surprised, Jackson stared at me before gently placing his glass on the counter, then sat back in his barstool, folded his arms and indicated he was giving me his full attention.

"Go on…" he nudged.

I looked around me to make sure that no-one else was listening in to our conversation, the way you do when you are feeling tipsy and think you are the beholder of the most secret information on the planet. Information that no-one else could give a damn about.

"Ok! only *I* could come all the way to New York and end up working beside my husband's pregnant ex, that's if she is his ex…. for all I know, they could still be together." *There, I had said it.*

Now it was Jackson's turn to shift uncomfortably from one foot to the next. I immediately picked up on his discomfort.

Alarmed, I grabbed his arm, unintentionally knocking the empty glass from his hand, causing it to smash into pieces on the bar floor. Everyone at the bar turned to stare.

"You know something. Don't you?" I heard my voice rise in pitch,

Embarrassed that I had brought attention to him, Jackson made his apologies to the barwoman as he kicked the shards of glass into a neat pile in front of the bar. He turned to face me, ready to impart an important piece of information, something he had been keeping to himself for a while.

"Willow, you do know she's going to fight you for him…you know that, don't you?" Jackson gently rubbed the top of my hand, as if trying to reassure me.

After a day like today, I had pretty much guessed that this would be the case. Jackson continued to stare at the glum expression on my face.

"She's not going to give Rick up just like that," he snapped his fingers. "She told me so. They were together an age before he met you," he paused, "And now…what with her carrying his baby," he paused as the words 'his baby' sank in, "Well, she's going to do everything in her power to get him back."

I felt defeated before the fight had even begun. A sick feeling rose in my belly.

"Damn him! Why did he walk into my life and cause all this chaos?"

"Because you attracted him in. That book you're always reading—what's it called? "You Only Get One Life—"

I finished the sentence for him, "Here's How to Live It."

"Yeah! That's the one!" He rounded on me, smiling wickedly, "Just a suggestion…. maybe you should put the book away… I mean don't take this the wrong way, but it doesn't seem to be doing you much good, does it?"

Then he went to the bathroom, leaving me alone with my thoughts.

8

BIG REVEAL

"Another round please."

Jackson had taken over 20 minutes to return from the Gents, leaving me alone to stare at the pitiful reflection looking up at me from the bottom of my glass.

Decidedly ahead of him in the drinking stakes, I stood up and pushed my barstool away deftly with one foot while crunching broken glass with the other.

"I've been thinking," I declared in tipsy fashion, hands on hips and full of bravado.

Trying his best to contain his amusement, Jackson gave me an encouraging smile, "Go on then…"

Clearing my throat for maximum dramatic effect, I announced again, "I've been thinking…if it wasn't for that book as you call it, I wouldn't be standing on broken glass in this gorgeous New York dive bar." The sound of broken glass underfoot only served to highlight my storyline to maximum effect.

Jackson looked like he was fit to burst, which only spurred me on further.

"If it wasn't for *THAT BOOK*, as you like to call it, I would be walking home alone along Buchanan Street on a freezing cold November night, after having spent an awful day at work, to spend the rest of the night alone in my room while my flat mate drunkenly entertained young men I went to school with in the front room."

"OK, OK, I get it. You're just yet another escapologist somehow hoping that New York is the answer to all your problems."

Shit! Is that what I am? An escapologist?

Turning the conversation back to Jackson, I enquired, "So, what about you then? What are you escaping from?"

Jackson grabbed me playfully by the wrist, guiding me back to the barstool as he stared me straight in the eyes. "Now that, my dear, is a long story…and sometime, maybe not too far from now, I might just tell you all about it. But for now, drink up! I have to get you home before it gets any later."

Frustrated with him withholding information from me, I was determined to find out more about him.

"OK then, Mr. Mysterious…if you weren't a makeup artist what would you be?" I asked.

"Oh…that's easy!" he replied, "I would have been a Flight Attendant."

"Really? For sure?" His answer took me by surprise. "Why?"

"The beautiful men, flying the globe, staying in fancy hotels…I mean, what's not to love?" he asked as a cheeky grin flashed across his face.

"Er…well, there's the jet lag, cranky passengers, screaming babies, long delays, and passengers throwing up in paper bags" I reminded.

Jackson put his glass down and regained a serious demeanour.

"You have to learn to look more on the bright side, Willow, you know…the world is an exciting place. Don't let your past tell you otherwise."

He was right. In so many ways, he was right.

"But enough about me…what about you? What would you be?" he asked, prodding my arm with his manicured finger.

"Oh, that's easy," I replied. "I would have been a makeup artist to the stars."

"Really? So, why are you still working behind the counter?" he asked, a cheeky glint appearing as he spoke.

I felt uncomfortable. *He's right—why have I not moved on from behind the counter?*

I shifted in my seat as I thought of a suitable answer.

"I suppose I just never got the chance," I said, annoyed with myself.

"Rubbish!" he declared. "You make your own luck in this life!" Jackson wagged his finger in my face. "Don't wait on someone coming along to save you—they'll never arrive. You've got to get out there and grab every opportunity that comes along."

"Yeah! You're right Jackson," I conceded, feeling slightly downcast and annoyed with myself.

Jackson sensed the change in mood.

"Look. Don't be so hard on yourself," Jackson rubbed my back. "You made it to New York, didn't you? Now that's no easy feat! Most people would never dream of marrying a guy after only six weeks…but you did!"

I looked up to see Jackson laughing at me. He was winding me up and winning.

"Cheeky!" I said as I playfully tapped him on the arm

Not ready for our bonding session to be over, I decided to jump right in with my size sevens and offered him some assistance.

"Look, I've been thinking about your counter."

"Have you now?" he asked, throwing his shoulder into his overcoat. "So, now you think you can save *me*?"

I ignored his sarcasm.

"Well… you and I could work on that counter together. Mrs. G asked me to figure out a way of helping you to increase sales. She thinks we should milk our "Britishness." We could really turn it around – put on posh accents, serve Earl Grey tea with a splash of lemon, and offer cucumber sandwiches to our customers. Oh, with the crusts cut off, of course!" I smiled, pleased with my own creative ideas. I could sense he was mulling over my suggestions.

Jackson stopped what he was doing and stared at me.

"She asked *you* to help *me* out?" Jackson appeared crestfallen like he had just been kicked in the stomach.

"…er, yeah…just in the short term, till you get back on your feet."

This wasn't going as well as I had anticipated. I was excited that my new boss had asked me to assist a colleague, but I could see the news was making Jackson feel insecure. I had to figure out a way to make him feel better.

"We could re-launch Luella Bee's Apothecary, you know…put a British twist on it! Call it Blake's Apothecary or something," I suggested, suddenly feeling excited about my prospects.

Jackson thought things over for a few moments. I could sense his cogwheels slowly churn as he digested my idea while I grew more and more excited by the idea's potential.

"You could sell the organic skincare, "I said, taking a deep breath, "and I'll encourage the women of Queens to ditch the orange skin and fake eyelashes and venture out without 7 inches of Pan Stick and spackle caked on their faces."

"You mean, promote the anti-Kardashian effect?" Jackson asked. "You're a riot!" He rolled his eyes, "Like, that'll ever happen! Not in this neck of the woods."

I listened to him, sighed, and slapped the table. "But we could give it a bloody good try!" I declared. I took mental stock, working the scenario out in my head. "I can just picture it now, no orange skin, no fake nails, and no triple-decker false eyelashes! What will the women of Queens think of that?" I asked, staring hard at Jackson.

"Ok," Jackson nodded. "I think you might be on to something here." He wore a serious business-like expression, one that hinted at past success.

"We could call it the "Great British Make-Under". The New York press will go apeshit for it." His blue eyes lit up like a light bulb as I sat back on my barstool, nodding in agreement.

"Well?" I enquired, looking up at him, expectation writ large across my eyes.

"Well, what?"

"What do we do now?" I asked.

"We dance!"

Jackson grabbed me again by the wrist, pulling me from my barstool as the first bars of Primal Scream's "Don't Fight It, Feel It" started to play over the bar's sound system. To my astonishment, and the amazement of everyone else at the bar, he began a series of intricate pirouettes, spins and leaps across the tiny dance floor. I trailed clumsily behind him as he dragged me by the wrist, and shouted into his ear, "Where did you learn to dance like that?" The pounding beat reverberated all around the tiny dance floor as Denise Johnson belted out, "Gonna get high till the day I die." Taking this as his cue, Jackson expertly picked me up and swung me around as if I was a slightly built rag doll.

"The Royal Ballet!" he shouted as I gasped at the very thought of him spinning me around one more time. Then, as quickly as the music had begun, I noticed a regretful expression take root on Jackson's face. Jackson let me go and gathered up our belongings before indicating towards the doorway.

"C'mon Cinderella. Better get you back to your husband before it gets any later."

I laughed. No one had ever referred to me as Cinderella before.

***

Jackson and I walked on in silence. Both of us deep in thought. As we neared the entrance to Rick's apartment building, I was more than a little thankful for him walking me home, considering the amount of alcohol we had consumed in the bar.

Our "goodbyes" were short and sweet as my new colleague made attempts to hail a cab back to his apartment. The yellow cab pulled up to the side of the pavement. Jackson cracked a smile, as his laughter lines crinkled.

"See you tomorrow then?" he chirped, winking at me.

Jackson folded his tall body into the back seat of the yellow cab. I could tell he had a lot on his mind…and so did I. Something made me look back, as the cab spun off into the darkness. That's when I saw him staring back at me. He waved.

Goodnight Jackson.

Five minutes later, as I stood outside the doorway of my new marital home, I put the key in the lock and opened the door to Rick's apartment. Peering in, I switched on the hallway light. Immediately, I was struck by the absence of the familiar musty smell that I had become accustomed to, this time my nostrils were happily greeted by the sweetest fragrance of pink peonies.

My favourite flowers!

Next to the bouquet of fresh-cut pink peonies lay a small, white, thickly embossed card with the words, "Hope you like the flowers. See you at 9pm," carefully etched across the front. I threw the card back on the counter and threw myself down on the couch.

I really wanted a fag. Maybe it was the alcohol but all I could think about was smoking a cigarette. I didn't understand this phenomenon at all. I had never smoked a cigarette in my life but right now there was nothing I wanted more than to light up and take a long drag.

Sitting there, looking around my surroundings, I decided the apartment could do with a quick furniture change and sprucing up before Rick got home. There wasn't much room to do anything substantial, but my years of reading "Elle Deco" had taught me some classic room layouts that would make a small space appear larger. I rolled up my sleeves and went to work. I moved the couch away from the wall and set the glass coffee table in the centre of the living room, opposite the faux fireplace. I lit the candles on top of the mantel and set my bouquet of pink peonies in a baby blue ceramic jug and placed the jug on top of a pile of glossy magazines. They weren't my type of magazine; they were mainly focused on financial issues and the stock market, which makes sense seeing as Rick worked in the Financial District of NYC. I would soon swap those out for a batch of glossy Vogue and interior design magazines. Rick's bachelor pad furniture was sleek and minimal, but I had already got my eye on some nice sage green velvet cushions on sale in the store. I would purchase them with my staff discount. That would salve the pain of the $30 price tag.

The galley kitchen was in dire need of some re-organisation. I made a mental note to buy six storage jars and printed labels as I earmarked a cabinet that could be turned into a pantry for dry goods. In the meantime, I moved the position of the new kettle to a countertop under the window then I set out a tray filled with accoutrements for making tea. My spirits lifted with every design decision…or was it the alcohol? Who knows? Whatever it was, it felt like my artistic touches were helping to soften Rick's testosterone-fueled design scheme. Smiling to myself, I poured myself a large glass of robust red wine and threw myself, once again, down on the couch. Scanning the room and feeling pleased with my interior design efforts, I raised my glass to no one in particular and called out, "Just needed a woman's touch, Ricky Boy."

As I squished into the couch, my attention was drawn to a small silver earring that had got stuck down the side of the seat cushion. I pulled it out and examined it carefully. It was an elegant design with a diamond stone.

My stomach lurched as I held yet another reminder of Rick's past in my sweaty palm. Deflated, I threw the earring into the cut glass plate on the coffee table and knocked back the wine in one big despondent glug.

That bloody woman is everywhere!

The nagging thoughts resumed their tirade.

Should have given it more time, Willow…Getting married? After only six weeks? You must be off your head.

Oh, shut the hell up!

As my mood became more morose, I thought of my choices: I could return home to my old life and pretend like this farce of a marriage never happened or I could stick it out, separate from Rick, and make it on my own. There was just one major problem with that scenario, without a spousal visa, I would be kicked out of the country and sent on my merry way.

My thoughts wouldn't leave me in peace. I was going to have to pick up the phone and tell Geneviève what has happened. Putting aside our differences, I reached over and dialed her number.

Don't pick up. Don't pick up. Don't pick up.

"Hello? Who is it?"

Shit! She picked up.

"Hi doll" I said, "It's me, Willow."

As I relayed the story of my arrival in New York to Geneviève, I couldn't quite believe it was Rick I was talking about.

"I told you this would happen. Now, didn't I?" she said in her trademark self-congratulatory tone.

"Yes. You did," I replied, feeling as small as a five-year-old child, "And you were right."

"If I were you, I would book a flight right now and come home!"

she demanded. "I'm not on best terms with the girl who has your room, so I'll kick her out and you can have your old room back...it'll be fun! Just like the old days!"

"Yes," I paused, unsure of myself, "I'll book a flight first thing in the morning."

Just as I replaced the phone on the receiver, the key turned in the lock. It was Rick.

"Hi!" Rick said, immediately changing his expression when he saw me. "What's the matter?" Rick asked, a concerned look appeared across his features.

"Er nothing. Nothing," I replied, shifting my weight uncomfortably on the couch.

"Have you been drinking?" Rick asked, his look appearing from one of concern to disapproval.

Once again, I felt like a small child being scolded for doing something wrong.

"Just one," I lied. "Jackson and I went for a cocktail after work." I looked up at Rick who was staring down at me, but I gathered up the strength to proceed on, "I've just spoken to Geneviève and I've decided to go home."

Rick threw his copy of the New York Financial Times on the couch as an exasperated look stretched across his face.

"Oh, don't be so stupid! You can't go home. You just got here."

This reply got my back up.

"Don't you dare call me stupid, Rick Delgado!" bolstered by alcohol, I stood up and faced him squarely, asserting myself in the room. "I'm not the stupid one in this scenario – you are!" He wasn't going to talk down to me, not when he was the one who was in the wrong. "I'm the one who has to go into work every day and face the humiliation of working alongside that bitch of an ex-girlfriend! Oh, and by the way, I found more of her belongings when I was moving the furniture around."

Rick looked sheepish as I handed him the earring.

"I had a past before you, Willow!" He shook the earring, "I didn't live like a bloody monk."

"I get that!" I said, "But none of this makes me feel any better, does it?"

Rick turned and stared at me.

"So what? All this time, you were just using me to get into the States. Is that it?" he asked meanly as if the thought of my imminent departure had finally sunk in.

"How long are you planning on going home for?" he asked, eyebrows raised in anticipation of my answer.

"I don't know," I responded. It was the truth. I had no idea how long I would go home for.

"But…You don't get it, Willow, if you were to leave now, they'll not let you back in."

Now it was my turn to be exasperated. "What do you mean "they won't let me back in"?""

Rick hurriedly rifled through a batch of legal documentation in our Green Card file and pulled out an important-looking document. He scanned the paper for a few seconds, then began to read, "It says here "If you leave the United States while your application is awaiting a decision from USCIS, your application will be considered abandoned, and in most cases, you will be required to refile your application upon return to the United States"…if they let you back in!" He went on, "And it says here, "Applicants must bear in mind that a re-entry permit does not guarantee them re-entry into the United States.""

Now I felt trapped. "But this can't be right…surely not?!" Panic was rising in my voice.

I threw myself down on the couch next to him, "What am I going to do Rick? This is impossible. I never knew any of this stuff."

Rick attempted to placate me, "It's just the way things are…I've heard of folks not being able to return home to say their final goodbyes. It's the price you have to pay if you want to live here permanently." He ruffled the top of my hair while looking off into the distance. The tears that had been mounting finally broke. Rick held me, whispering in my ear, "You wanted this lifestyle babe. This is the price you have to pay."

I looked up at him, "Is that all you can say? This is the price I have to pay?"

His words struck me as cold, and unfeeling. I pulled away from him. It was alright for him; he would never have to make a decision like the one I was going to have to make.

I got up and left the living room, slamming the door shut behind me. I wanted to get away…to just breathe…be on my own while I figured everything out in my head. But there was no escape. Rick followed me into the bedroom.

"You should have done your homework, Willow. This is just the way things are. They're not going to bend the rules so you can run off whenever you feel like it. They don't care what the reason is."

I glared back at him, seething. I took out my phone and pressed the "confirmation" button on the British Airways flight reservation screen. My flight home was now booked, and I shook the screen in Rick's direction.

The colour left his face as he scowled at me, turned around, and slammed the door shut.

I instantly regretted my decision.

Bloody hell! What a fucking mess this is!

9

EXFOLIATOR

Mrs. G's morning meetings always ran like clockwork. D'Arcy's Department Store didn't open till 10 am but all personnel were expected to be standing behind their counters, looking perfectly groomed and ready for the day's business at 9:45 sharp. I arrived at 9:40 to the sound of Michael Bublé crooning sweet nothings from the store speakers. Mornings mostly consisted of everyone sharing little bits of gossip between the counters as they prepped their makeup and made last-minute touch-ups before facing the day. Today was no different, and I heard a few of the assistants gossiping about someone named Chi-Chi who was on maternity leave. As soon as Mrs. G made her appearance, an eerie silence swept over the shop floor as she captured her staff's attention. One deft clap of her hand was all it took.

"Good morning ladies and gentlemen," she stated.

"Good morning Mrs. G," a few of the staff responded in unison.

"Today, I have some exciting news for you!" she beamed.

Everyone exchanged glances. I saw a few of my colleagues visibly brace themselves for what was about to come next. I suspected that a lot of them had been in the business for a long time and were not exactly welcoming of change.

"Would Willow Campbell-Delgado and Jackson Dart please step forward?" Mrs. G looked straight at us as I felt the colour rise in my cheeks. Jackson glanced at me; his expression unreadable.

Now it was our turn to exchange glances as we both timidly stepped out into the middle of the shop floor to face Mrs. G. I could see some of the women's reflections in Dior's counter mirrors as Jackson and I contemplated our fates.

"I've been observing you both for a while now and…"

My heart missed a beat as I eyed Jackson out of the corner of my eye.

Oh, my dear God, I'm going to be fired.

"Willow, don't look so worried!" Mrs. G forced out a laugh. "I've decided I'd like to see you both work together on the brand new "Blake's Apothecary" counter." Mrs. G shot me a wry smile as she spoke.

Jackson winked at me and then it clicked. Our conversation from the previous night had already made its way to Mrs. G. I felt annoyed that I hadn't been asked to take part in any discussion.

When did he find the time to chat with her?

"I've agreed on a meeting with the head of Marketing for 11:00 tomorrow morning and Maria is very excited to hear your ideas for the counter."

I made eye contact with Mrs. G as she emphasised the word "ideas." I felt myself shake. It was now or never.

***

"Er …"

My hands were soaked in sweat as I clasped them tightly behind my back.

Mrs. G stared hard at me, urging me to go on. Making me feel like I was wasting her valuable time.

"I, er, I can't make it." *There. I've said it.*

I felt Jackson's scowl cut through me like a blade even though I daren't look at him.

"I'm leaving, tonight."

God. He must hate me.

"Home? To Scotland?" Mrs. G stared at me as I tried to avoid Jackson's icy gaze. I nodded in agreement. Mrs. G appeared to pale as she paused for a second.

"I thought I made it clear that if you go home now during this part of your Green Card application that it's highly likely you won't get back in again?" she asked, staring at me, incredulous that I had even expressed a wish to leave. "Well?" she enquired, anticipating my response.

I looked down at my shoes. I gulped hard. I sweated. But I said nothing.

"Then I'll have to replace you," she stated.

I'll have to replace you.

I noticed a cruel smirk break out on Isabella's face as my stomach lurched.

Mrs. G's words stung me. Icy, brutal, without compassion. Bringing a flurry of bad memories to the surface.

I was used to being replaced. From the moment my parents were killed in the horrific car accident at the foot of the Pentland hills till the time I reached adulthood, being replaced was a common theme running through my life. As hard as I tried, I just couldn't seem to fit in. Always looking inward from the periphery, wishing that I was one of those people who could swan through life with ease. Then when boys came on the scene, that theme continued. One by one, I always seemed to be replaced by girls who were prettier than I was.

Jackson pulled me aside, a few steps away from Mrs. G.

"You can't go Willow…I'll be out of a job if you go!" he pleaded with me.

Staring at me; silently questioning me; pinning all his hopes on me.

Don't do this to me, I silently pleaded back.

I wondered just what kind of deal he had struck with Mrs. G in the early hours of the morning. Whatever had happened, I felt truly awful. Leaving New York had been the last thing on my mind.

"I know how this must all look," I blurted out. "I just need to get away for a while." I stared over at Isabella as I spoke.

Mrs. G immediately took a step back as the workers on the shop floor all turned and stared at Isabella. Isabella cupped her growing belly in her manicured hand. Her complexion glowing with pregnancy hormones as a self-satisfied smirk stretched across her face.

"Oh, well I am sorry to hear that," she hesitated then blurted, "But are you sure you are doing the right thing?"

Appearing uncharacteristically ill-at-ease, my boss caught herself mid-sentence.

"I expect you are," she pulled at her shirt sleeve,

Now it was my turn to placate.

"It's OK," I replied. "It's fine, really."

Deep inside, I felt chilled to the bone. My thoughts ran amok as the burden of my decision began to weigh heavily on me.

Looking up into Jackson's face, I could tell immediately that he wasn't buying it.

"Think about it Willow, Mrs. G is right," Jackson said quietly, looking down at his shoe. "And I'm not being selfish here, but you really must think this through before getting on that flight tonight."

I sensed that Jackson was fighting not only for his job but for his career.

Oh my God, I feel bloody awful! Damned if I do, damned if I don't.

My heart pounded violently in my chest. These people had only just come into my life, so why did I feel pulled in every direction? Rick wasn't talking to me. He told me that if I were to get on that airplane, our marriage would be over. I could feel the familiar sensation of tears bubbling under the surface, the lump in my throat…threatening to ruin my composure.

Not now. Keep it together Willow. Keep it together.

Mrs. G expertly diagnosed the situation. "Jackson, take Willow to the staff room and get her some coffee please," she ordered. As we walked past, I overheard her whisper in his ear, "Get her to think about this. This is serious." Out of the corner of my eye, I saw Isabella stare over. Her expression unnerved me; she looked like the cat that had just got the cream.

Jackson and I stood opposite each other in the staff room. Neither of us knew what to say or do as we held our plastic cups of machine sludge coffee. Strangely, I felt like it was me who should be doing the comforting and not the other way around. No matter what I did, I would be letting someone down, and on top of everything, I still had the fallout from the previous night's argument with Rick to deal with.

"What time is your flight?" Jackson asked, shoulders sunken in defeat.

"11pm. I'm almost packed. Just a few last things to throw in my case."

"How's Rick taking the news?"

"He's not," I replied, looking away from Jackson.

"Yeah…I can see his point. Look…you *will* think about staying?" Jackson pleaded as he put his arm around me.

"Promise," I attempted a smile in his direction but both of us knew I was merely placating him. Inside, I felt like I was being sliced open by a knife. Everything was black and white; there was no grey area. The action I was about to take would have an immense impact on my future. I gazed into my new friend's eyes as tears threatened to spill over my freshly applied makeup. We didn't say a word.

The irony of Frank Sinatra singing "That's Life" was not lost on me. D'Arcy's Department Store was once again open for business.

***

Eyes dried and composure regained, Jackson led the way as we walked back to our counters. No one dared look at me as I walked past. As I stepped nearer my counter, I noticed Isabella staring straight at me. That's when it struck me, I was playing right into her hands.

Back at my counter, I worked hurriedly through a pile of paperwork – tallying up targets for the day, calculating percentages, and working out the amount of product to shift per hour. My brain whirred erratically as I tried not to compute ways in which my decision would affect those closest to me.

"That's her over there."

I looked up from my paperwork to see Jackson being questioned by a man in uniform. He was pointing in my direction. A sense of unease washed over my body. Exasperated, I threw my pen down.

Oh God! What now?

I swallowed hard.

What the f? Who is this guy and why is he walking in my direction?

I put the paperwork away as Mrs. G sidled up to my counter arriving at the same time as the uniformed man.

"Can I be of help, Officer?" asked Mrs. G pleasantly, granting me a sideways look that indicated she was now in control.

Seemingly unaffected by the presence of a strong, beautiful woman standing in front of him, the officer held up his badge, displaying it for both of us to see.

"Homeland Security."

"I see," Mrs. G replied, equally visibly unmoved by his display of authority.

"I'm here to question Willow Campbell-Delgado," the officer stared at me as he spoke. I shivered.

"Is there somewhere private we can go?" the officer's voice was gruff. "I need to ask your *employee* here a few questions."

I didn't appreciate the emphasis he placed on the word "*employee*." I looked over in Jackson's direction, but he was gone already; so was Isabella.

Mrs. G indicated for the officer and I to follow her, "Come with me, you can use my office."

This is all very suspicious, I thought. As the three of us entered Mrs. G's office, she motioned for both the officer and I to sit down. The officer declined, leaving me to sit alone at the table in front of Mrs. G. I hadn't known her very long but the expression on her face was telling and summed up that there was way more to her than just this austere "in control" image she presented to the outside world.

"And so young lady… it says here—in my notes—that you are married to a Mr. Ricardo Delgado? Is that correct?" the officer stared hard at me, refusing to give anything away in his expression. I could tell he was "an old hat" at his job.

"Yes, that's correct," I replied, staring straight back at him. *I'm tougher than you think mister.*

"And where did you get married?" he asked, as he fiddled with his well-chewed biro.

"Cléments Estate, Loch Lomond," I answered, looking him straight in the eye, wondering why the hell I was being questioned in the first place.

The officer looked over at Mrs. G with a confused look on his face, "What did she just say? I didn't catch a word of that."

The bloody cheek of him!

Mrs. G looked over in my direction, a faint smile creeping around the edges of her perfectly penciled mouth. "That's funny officer, I got it all. She said Clements Estate, Loch Lomond. Now Loch Lomond is in a beautiful part of Scotland, and for your information, Scotland is part of the United Kingdom…well, it was the last time I checked on CNN, but that situation may have changed by now."

You go, Mrs. G! I wanted to hug her.

"I got it," the officer quipped sternly, scribbling furiously in his little black notebook while I pinched myself in an attempt to stop laughing. I daren't look at Mrs. G.

"Show me her paperwork," he demanded.

Mrs. G slowly and silently got up from her chair and opened her pristine filing cabinet, which was filled with paperwork all meticulously labelled in baby blue ink. Shooting me a warning look, she handed my file to the officer and sat back down on her sheepskin covered Philippe Starck Ghost Chair. I gripped the side of my seat, mentally preparing myself for the next set of questions.

Who would have thought working as a makeup artist in New York would be such a white-knuckle ride?

I was completely unprepared for the next question.

"How long did you know Ricardo Delgado prior to marrying him?"

I glanced over my shoulder and looked at Mrs. G. It was as if we both instantly knew where this line of questioning was going. "Em…"

Right girl. Take it slowly. Breathe.

"About six weeks." I stated defiantly.

"Six weeks you say?" he re-iterated.

I stared at my shoes as the officer chuckled to himself. The way this was all panning out, he may as well just have shouted "Game Over." The confidence I felt earlier evaporated in an instant.

"And you're how old?" he asked, "28 years old according to this paperwork?" the officer droned on, going through the motions Mrs. G nudged me under the table, urging me to answer.

"Er yes." I looked at Mrs. G as she shifted uncomfortably in her chair.

What's she playing at? Changing my age to 28!

Why did she put me down as 28? Is there some age discrimination going on here? I thought. *I'm 33 on my next birthday.*

Looking up from my feet, I stared the officer in the eyes, "What exactly are you getting at?"

"What I am getting at, Mrs. Campbell-Delgado, is that perhaps you might have seen one last opportunity to escape your miserable life and you took it…Am I right?" his right cheek sidled up in a mocking smirk as he continued to pencil notes in his little black book.

"No! It wasn't like that at all!" I shouted, strangely unnerved by my own defensive reaction to his line of questioning.

Deep down though, if I was really, really honest with myself…my heart sank as even I couldn't bring myself to contemplate what I had done. The truth hurt. He had hit the nail on the head, but that didn't stop me from wanting to stand up and slap him.

I caught Mrs. G and the officer exchanging a look. In finality, the officer closed his notebook, then made his way to the office door. I remained in my chair, feeling like I had just taken a punch to the stomach.

Placing one hand on the door, he turned around to fire one more parting shot, "That'll be all for today. We *will* be taking our investigations further. Let your *husband* know that we will be paying him a visit. I take it you do live together?"

"Of course we do."

Fuck!.

10

COLOUR CORRECTOR

That evening as the winter moonlight glinted through the vertical blind slats, I watched as Rick made up a bed on the couch. He threw a pile of pillows and blankets unceremoniously on the floor as he huffed and puffed, making it known to me in a non-verbal fashion, that he was at best displeased with me and at worst, absolutely furious. Our short time together made it impossible for me to surmise which one it was. The stellar scene outside our window only heightened the tense and morose atmosphere inside apartment 168, Manhattan Heights. He hadn't spoken to me since our discussion earlier, and it felt like you could cut the atmosphere with a knife. I traipsed around the apartment, silently picking up my last few remaining belongings as he lay on the couch hiding behind a copy of the New York Financial Times.

I couldn't help feeling that everything had ended before it had even begun. Since our arrival, there had been no romantic flowering of our relationship, instead, we had been dumped into a melee of lies and deceit – the very stuff I had been hoping to escape.

Wanting to break away from the tension in the room, I entered the en-suite and quietly jammed the lock shut. Standing in front of the bathroom mirror, I felt the tears threaten to well up, but this time I allowed them to fall down my face and splash into the sink below. I noticed the shadows around my eyes were growing darker by the day and no matter how much concealer I applied, those annoying stretches of darkness still managed to peek out from behind their cashmere canvas.

Bloody waste of time and money; another product I've been suckered into buying that doesn't work.

Ironically, it was one of my best-selling items on the counter. I scraped my nail across a dried-in foundation ring on the windowsill, one that had somehow missed the vigorous Windex onslaught. Staring at the speckles of foundation that now lay inside my nail extension, I thought back to how Isabella must have felt that evening when she got the call from Rick telling her to vacate the apartment. Now, it's my turn to leave his apartment.

***

"Bang! Bang! Bang!"

What the …?

"Bang! Bang!"

I leaped out the bathroom and made my way to the bedroom as Rick answered the door.

"Mr. Delgado? Homeland Security, may we come in?" Officer Jamieson had warned me they would turn up, but just before 7:00pm on a Friday? This was bloody ridiculous!

Eyeballing the three men through the gap between the door and the doorframe, I watched as the shorter of the two officers began scribbling notes in a small notebook. I followed his eyes as he looked intently at the bedding on the couch, then at Rick.

"Oh, that?" I heard him say, "I snore. Real bad. My wife makes me sleep on the couch."

You go, Rick! Good on you!

The shorter man carried on writing notes while Mr. Jamieson assumed a more aggressive stance in front of Rick. I had to give it to my husband, he stood his ground, standing there in his flannel pj bottoms with striped bedraggled t-shirt hanging off one shoulder. The other financial hot shots on Wall Street would be in fits if they could see him right now.

"I spoke with your wife earlier today, is she here?"

Shit! Shit! Shit!

I ran towards my bed and jumped in under the covers, just as my husband and the two Homeland Security Officers entered the room.

Fuck!

My heart pounded in my chest as beads of sweat formed on my forehead. It was hot under the covers. I couldn't see what they were doing, but I could hear Rick answer, "Of course she is, she's taking a nap, hang on…I'll just wake her, OK?"

"Please," replied Officer Jamieson.

As I pretended to be asleep under the bedcovers, the adrenaline forcing through my veins caused flashes of sweat to soak my back. Rick pulled back the heavy bed cover, "Get up Willow. These men want to talk to us." I had never seen my new husband look so serious.

"Er… Hello again Mr. Jamieson!" I blushed. Mortified that I was lying in bed fully clothed.

"Hello, Mrs. Campbell-Delgado. Nice to see you again." He looked over at Rick as he spoke, "I'm assuming your *wife* did tell you we would be visiting?"

Cheeky git!

I hated how he put the emphasis on the word "wife."

Rick drew me a foul look, "She did indeed…although I wasn't expecting a visit at this time on a Friday night. You guys not in a hurry to get to the bar?" Rick asked, with an air of nonchalance. That question annoyed me. Why couldn't he be serious when dealing with people in a position of authority? Although his mighty self-confidence was one of the qualities that attracted me to him in the first place.

Mr. Jamieson declined to join in with the small talk.

"We operate a 24/7 service, sir. You can expect a visit from us at any time of the day or night," he responded smugly.

With Rick put firmly back in his place, the second officer walked towards him holding a piece of paper in his hand. He had picked it up off the bedroom floor. Apparently, Rick had written me a note while I was in the bathroom.

"What's this then?" he asked before reading out the scrawled words on the note.

"*We're invited to dinner at my mom's tomorrow night. Can't you stay for one more day and act like you're my wife.*"

Rick replied, "But you don't understand Officer, that note was written in anger."

It was quite clear that the game was up. The two officers stared at me while Rick gazed helplessly at his bare feet. The smaller officer placed the note carefully in a plastic bag then sealed it, while Officer Jamieson stared down at me.

"We'll see ourselves out. Expect to hear from us again in a few days."

Hauling myself up, I attempted to smooth my bed hair and regain my composure while Rick continued to stare at his feet.

"And you, *Mrs.* Delgado,"

I didn't like the way he emphasised the "Mrs." bit.

"You have a good night!" said the officer.

"It's Campbell-Delgado actually," I responded, somehow finding the courage to look right through him.

Correcting him, I was painfully aware of my inability to think of anything clever to say.

As the apartment door slammed shut, Rick threw himself face down on the bed and let out a groan.

"I don't understand any of this! Why don't they believe us, Rick?"

Looking up at me, his face gnarled in an expression I had never seen before, Rick placed his hands on my hands and stared at me.

"Believe us?" he gasped, "I'm in this marriage and even I don't believe it! Seven days to gather evidence from everyone who knows us? What the fuck! Seven days to prove that we have a legitimate marriage and here you are, heading off to stay with an old flat mate who doesn't even like you, for fuck's sake, Willow."

I held my head in the palms of my sweaty hands, feeling emotionally and physically drained by what had just happened. I had never heard him sound so angry.

But deep down, if I was really, honest with myself, I knew his words rang true.

Refusing to take onboard his viewpoint of my dysfunctional relationship with Geneviève, I stood in front of him, hands on hips and declared, "I've got to get packed."

As I made to exit the room, Rick grabbed me by the wrist as he lay on his stomach, "Look, you're the only one for me," he pleaded, despair welling in his eyes.

Turning my face away from his, my stomach lurched. *Don't do this. Please don't do this to me.*

"Willow, you're the only one for me. When I was with Isabella, I thought I was in love with her...then I met you, that's when I realised what *real* love is," Rick remonstrated as I observed a single bead of sweat run down the side of his face.

Keep it together Willow.

"That night in that restaurant in Scotland, two weeks after I met you...I called her and told her we were over."

Placing my feet squarely on the sheepskin rug, I turned to face him. I wanted to believe him, but I felt so conflicted. He gripped my wrist and held on tightly, staring at me with a pleading expression, as if his very life depended on me staying in New York. Ignoring the despair in his eyes, I drew upon my last ounce of inner strength.

"Really? I hear it, but I don't see it. I've been such a bloody fool…silly…childish…living in a dream world, running all the way over here to be with you and look where it got us…visits from the authorities and the daily indignity of working with your ex. It's hardly the perfect start to a new life in America, is it? And then I find out your "ex" is pregnant with your child…it's hardly what I would call a reason to stay, is it?"

Rick glared furiously at me, "What did you expect Willow? Some fairyland? Somethin' out a storybook?" he snorted. "It's New York and now you're acting like your shit don't stink! Like nothing is good enough for you, and for the last time, that baby's not mine!" he shouted, frightening me.

"You told me you were bringing me to Manhattan! Not bloody Manhattan *Nights*…not some dump in the back of beyond."

There, I had said it. Said what I had been feeling all this time. I felt Rick's grip on my wrist loosen as my stand-up-for-myself speech sank in.

"You can hardly call Queens the "back of beyond" for Chrissakes, get a grip!" Rick huffed. "Anyway, what does it matter where you live, you're with me…is that not enough?"

I didn't respond. I looked away. He was right. He should be enough.

What's wrong with me?

Pulling my hand from his, I rubbed my hands as an angry red band appeared around my wrist.

I picked up the yellow book that had been lying on the bedside table and threw it unceremoniously into my fake Kelly bag,

"I'm done, Rick. I can't do this anymore. I'm going home."

Deflated, I pulled the suitcase down from the top of the closet, checked it for any signs of ant infestation, then threw in the few clothes I had brought with me. So much for shopping in Saks and Macy's and Nordstrom. My "American dream" had evaporated before I even had the chance to purchase my very first Kate Spade bag.

I heard Rick mutter under his breath, "This can't be happening." I stood aside as he made his way to the kitchen, refusing to look my way.

Stepping into the ensuite to get dressed, I wavered for a second before regaining my steely resolve. I noticed the last few remaining minute traces of red lipstick remained on the mirror, and despite Rick's protestations to the contrary, I realised that Isabella had very clearly not left the building.

***

Alone, I lugged the heavy suitcase from the top of the bed onto the floor and out into the living room. Willing myself to stay strong, I silently coached myself: *You can do this. You can do this. You can do this. Just look straight ahead. Don't look at him.*

Reaching the apartment door, I placed my sweat-soaked hand on the door handle, forcing myself not to look at Rick.

"I'll call you when I land," I whispered, knowing that if I spoke louder, emotions would cloud my words and I might be persuaded to stay.

I felt Rick's shallow breath on the back of my neck, his delicate touch on the small of my back.

I coached myself: *Keep it together. Don't look at him.*

"Won't you reconsider?" Silence. "Please, Willow, I'll do anything!" The depth of emotion in his voice unnerved me. I had never heard him sound so vulnerable.

This was unbearable.

Don't say anything. Keep going.

Burt Bacharach's "This guy's in love with you" played softly from the kitchen radio as if he was callously poking fun at our ridiculous relationship.

Go now! Just keep walking. Don't look back. Don't say anything.

I closed the apartment door gently behind me. I didn't look back. I rushed down the corridor as fast as I could go, willing Rick not to come after me. Then it struck me. If he didn't come after me, would he really give up so easily? I pressed the button to call the lift and immediately felt a rush of panic descend over me.

Was I really doing this? Was I really going back? Hurry up, lift. Get me out of here, quick!

The lift arrived just four seconds later but it felt like an eternity. Any minute now, Rick would appear and persuade me to go back to him. As the doors opened slowly, I rushed in rolling the heavy suitcase over my foot.

"Ouch!"

Frantically, I pressed the button over and over as the only other person in the lift, an older man in his late 50s, stared at me.

"Going somewhere nice?" he asked, a wicked smile leeching out of his gnarled face.

I ignored him. Praying instead that the door wouldn't suddenly open and reveal Rick standing there staring at me, but still half-hoping that it would.

Shit! This is awful.

A minute later, we reached the lobby. Grabbing the handle of my suitcase, I hobbled out of the tiny compartment as fast as I could, not daring to look behind me. Five minutes later, I was expertly hailing a cab like a native New Yorker and telling the driver to take me straight to JFK. As we sped off, I finally allowed myself to look back towards the apartment building, one last time. There was no sign of Rick.

11

RUNWAY

Thirty-five minutes later, I arrived at the British Airways check-in desk in JFK.

"Mrs. Campbell-Delgado, would you like a window or aisle seat?"

"Window, please."

"Seat 35A has just become available. I've blocked the seat next to it so you should have some room. Please go straight to security then proceed to Gate 12."

"Thanks," I muttered under my breath, as I tried to stall a burgeoning tear. I looked behind me at the remainder of the queue of passengers, all last-minute stragglers like me, but there was no sign of Rick. He hadn't bothered to come after me and make one last-ditch attempt to get me to stay. There was nothing left for me to do but to carry on with my journey.

Trudging through the airport, I stopped at a specialty bagel store. I had passed by one of these stores on the way to work every morning and had made a mental note to stop in one day and sample their fare. Now, seemed as good a time as any.

Five minutes later, a comforting cup of latte in hand, I chewed slowly on my lox bagel, savouring every mouthful. As the array of delicious flavours danced on my taste buds, my thoughts quickly returned to my first day in New York and how Rick had attempted to buy lunch for me at the Little Café in Central Park. Only a few short weeks ago, it was just me, Rick, a plateful of ciabatta bread, a bowl of olives and tapenade, and what seemed like all the time in the world to savour our brand-new life together. Except, there was one vital ingredient missing – Rick's wallet. The thought struck me, *had he mistakenly left his wallet in the apartment when he took the cases up? And why did he tell me he lived in Manhattan when the reality was a forlorn tower block in Queens. Why did he feel the need to impress me?*

***

"Would all remaining passengers flying to London Heathrow on BA 1515 please proceed now to Gate 12, where your flight is currently boarding."

Brushing away a stray lock of hair, I picked up my Kelly bag and took out the yellow book that was partly responsible for getting me into this mess in the first place. I took one last look at it before throwing it in the nearest trash bin.

There. That's where you belong.

Deep inside me, I knew that from now on, there would be no more need for such frivolous nonsense in my life. It was time to finally grow up and face the consequences of my rash actions.

Feeling emotionally bruised from my short time in New York, I prepared to return home to my old life in Scotland, the same life I had been so desperate to leave.

***

"Ahem! I think you forgot something."

I turned around to see Jackson smile down at me. He was holding a grubby yellow book in his hand.

"What are you doing here?" I asked, shocked to the core.

"I found this in the trash and knew you had to be around here somewhere," Jackson joked, then got serious. "I can't let you go through with this, Willow. I can't stand by and let you throw this opportunity away. It's too important. You can't go home…not now."

My head was swimming as my flight number was called out again. I felt a tear snake down my right cheek as the stress of the last few days took its toll on me. I never wanted to be in this position but what was I supposed to do? I looked up at Jackson, his kind smile revealing two rows of perfectly aligned sparkling white teeth.

"I don't have a choice. I can't stay with him," I blurted.

"There's always a choice, Willow. Come back with me," he said kindly, as he gently attempted to take the ticket and passport from me. "If you like, you can stay with me for a while, let everything calm down…then make a rational decision."

"This is a final call for Mrs. Willow Campbell-Delgado travelling to London Heathrow on BA 1515. Please go to gate 12 immediately."

"That's me! They're calling my name! I need to go, Jackson," I panicked as I took my ticket and passport from him.

"Willow!" Jackson shouted, exasperated, stopping me in my tracks. "Don't do this. You'll regret it for the rest of your life. Trust me. I know what I'm talking about."

"It's not that easy Jackson. I married him…and now he's having a baby with her…"

The floodgates burst their banks finally as Jackson stepped forward and wrapped his arms around me.

"I know…I know…it's shit," he cupped his hand under my chin and made me look at him. "I don't want you to make the same mistake I did. That's all. I want you to have time to think things through. You know…be my flat mate while the dust settles," he suggested

I laughed through the tears, "You just want me to help pay your electric bill, don't you?"

"Well," he paused, "there's that too!"

"This is the last and final call for Mrs. Willow Campbell-Delgado. Please go to Gate 12 where your flight is waiting to depart," the announcer was getting antsy.

I thought about Jackson's suggestion as the voice of reason in my head analysed the pros and cons of the situation. It would buy me some more time if I stayed a little longer plus there was the added attraction of not having to "eat humble pie" and return to my flat mate.

I looked up at Jackson, smiled, and finally relented.

"Ok. You've persuaded me," I said quietly, once again second-guessing the wisdom of my actions.

Jackson grinned from ear to ear.

He put his arm around me and walked me to the baggage desk.

"We need to get a suitcase offloaded," Jackson said to the agent behind the desk.

12

PORT WINE STAIN

Jackson and I made a detour to our favourite hangout – Lola's Bar. The one we visited every Thursday night. The day that officially signposted the way to the weekend.

He placed the large suitcase by the side of my feet while we took up our favourite position on the barstools. He ordered me a large glass of red wine and a Corona for himself. Then sat down next to me, staring at me.

"How did you know where to find me?" I asked.

"Rick called me," he stated.

"He did?" I asked, as I experienced a conflict of emotions overwhelm me.

"Whatever you think of him, Willow, he was messed up…in real bad shape, sobbing he was."

"No! Never!" I shook my head disbelieving. "Not Rick. I've only ever seen him cry over a £1000 lost bet in the bookies! You're making this stuff up."

Taking the huff, Jackson looked over my shoulder.

"Think what you will, but I'm guessing that guy really loves you," he responded, sulkily.

"But what about Isabella…and the baby?" I was seriously confused now.

"There's a good chance the baby's not his," he stated.

"But…how can you say that?" I asked.

"I was with Isabella the night before Rick left for Glasgow, they had a falling out, and we went out dancing…she went off with another guy at the end of the night."

Had I got it all wrong? Was he over Isabella? Now, I was delighted but still confused.

"You mean the baby might not be his?" I exclaimed as a swirl of thoughts and questions arose… *Does he really love me? Had I got it so wrong?*

"Will you take me back there? I want to see him," I asked, pulse racing.

Jackson brightened, "Of course I will." He nodded. "Hurry! Drink up. Let's go."

***

The streets of New York began to look vaguely familiar as I recognised landmarks along the way. I cast my memory back to how I felt when I first arrived in the city. I blushed at the memory of thinking I was going to be staying in uptown Manhattan, laughing at my own naiveté as I remembered standing in front of Manhattan Heights with the missing "H." Smiling at my own absurdness, my heart missed a beat as we pulled up in front of the dingy brown apartment building. Leaping out, I left it to Jackson to pay the fare. Catching my reflection in the mirrored lobby, I was thankful that Jackson had done an expert job on my makeup in the back seat of the taxi. Gone were the puffy eye bags and any tell-tale redness around the rims of my eyes had been camouflaged with a white pencil. He even did my hair – backcombing the roots and giving it some bounce, then he sprayed it into place with a tiny travel size canister of hairspray.

"Keep that in your bag," he said, handing me the canister, "It makes a great self-defense weapon." Then he looked around him,

"Especially in this neck of the woods."

But I was only half-hearing him as my mind was on other things: *Things are going to get better now. We'll make up and pretend like none of this ever happened. It will be a fresh start for both of us.*

I visualised myself settling down with Rick, enjoying my job in D'Arcy's and making a frenemy out of Isabella. After all, it was me who Rick really loved. He had told me so himself. Suddenly, Jackson's high-pitched, cut glass, London accent blasted into my thoughts.

"You go on ahead luv…I'll catch you up," he urged as he took out a packet of cigarettes and offered one to the cab driver.

Can't take you anywhere, can I? I shook my head, smiling.

Standing in the familiar surroundings of the lift, alone, I took a deep breath and pressed number 14. The return ticket would have to be cancelled and I would probably lose the money on it, but I would soon make it up on a couple of overtime shifts later in the month. Saving my marriage would take precedence over everything, of that I was sure.

As I stepped out of the lift and into the lobby, I waited a few moments to see if Jackson would catch up. I needed his presence to reassure me. After all, if he hadn't revealed that morsel of information, then I would not be standing in the very building I had left so dramatically only a few hours earlier.

The adjacent lift door opened to reveal a beaming Jackson. Noticing that I was waiting to "do my thing" and makeup with Rick, Jackson stepped forward and hugged me tightly.

"You go on ahead," he whispered encouragingly, "I'll wait back here for ten minutes and then if you don't come out…I'll see you at work tomorrow!" he winked.

"You sure?" I asked, not quite believing how well things were all panning out.

Throwing that yellow book away had to be one of the best things I'd ever done.

Now, I was making decisions all by myself and boy did it feel good to be in control.

"Yes! Now go! Go!" he urged, shooing me forward like a kid at primary school leaving their dad for the first time.

It was now or never.

Walking along the carpeted hallway, I heard soothing notes of Bossa Nova bouncing off the walls. The closer I got to the apartment, the louder the notes became as back-up singers sung, "Going out of my head."

I didn't know Rick liked Sergio Mendez ... That's a first. I'll have to buy him the album for Christmas.

The notes tinkled and reverberated, echoing soothingly along the corridor walls. I imagined Rick sitting on the couch, huddled over, full of remorse and clutching onto one of the last remaining crystal cut glass tumblers we received as a wedding present. I imagined the glass filled to the brim with the cloying amber nectar, product of my home country. Smiling warmly, I turned and looked back at Jackson. He gestured with his hands, urging me to go on and press the doorbell.

Taking a deep breath once again, I fixed my hair and smoothed my brows, then I knocked on the door, timidly at first. No one answered. I knocked again. Still nothing. I waited. Then, after what seemed like an eternity, I knocked once more but this time with more authority. The seductive tones of the music continued. I knocked again, much louder this time. *Surely, he would hear me now?*

I was right. The door cracked open slightly revealing a darkened hallway and only the side view of Rick's profile.

"Bella! Turn that music down!" Rick laughed and turned to face me, shock arising in his expression. "Willow! What are you doing here?" His tone changed dramatically.

I had heard everything I needed to hear. We stood face to face, staring at each other, both of us waiting for the other person to speak. I saw Bella rush towards the door, wearing a short pink satin dressing gown, tied loosely at the waist. Her feet were bare, and her eyeliner smudged. Seeing me, she sneered, "I thought you'd left?"

***

I've often heard that actions speak louder than words. That night, I had an out of body experience. I watched myself run. I ran down the lobby, past Jackson, and kept on running. I ran past the lift door and kept on running. Somehow, and I don't know how, I knew exactly where the fire escape was and so I ran, down —to floor ten, then 9, then 8, then 7, then 6, then 5, then 4, and my heart maintained a rhythmical beat. Ironically, the SugaBabes' "Round Round" lyrics filled my ears as I continued to floor 3, floor 2, and then floor 1. My lungs, parched of oxygen, felt like they might explode.

Then I saw myself fall into a strong pair of arms.

"Fuck him," Jackson said. "You're coming home with me."

13

SHOCK VALUE

Jackson settled me into his green-winged armchair in front of the fireplace then fetched me a mug of freshly boiled hot chocolate.

"Take this," he demanded, "It's good for the shock."

My hand wavered and shook as I wrapped my palm around the mug, heat searing into my hand. I sat there and watched on while Jackson scurried around collecting sheets, blankets, and pillows for a makeshift bed on the couch.

"I'll sleep here tonight, and you can have my bed till you figure out what you want to do next."

"That's kind of you," I whispered as one tear escaped down my cheek. "But I'm not taking your bed, you've already done more than enough for me. I'll sleep on the couch."

I climbed under the covers that draped over the couch. It was cold in his apartment. I guessed he wasn't a fan of turning on the heat while he was trying to survive in New York City on our wages.

"If you get hungry during the night, you'll find some cheese and crackers on a plate in the fridge," Jackson said.

I smiled meekly, "Thanks Jackson, you're too kind."

I gulped down the last dregs of the hot chocolate as Jackson switched off the lights.

"Night Jackson."

"Night Willow."

It was a relief to finally be in pitch darkness, where no-one could see me, as I sobbed myself to sleep.

***

I awoke early the next morning to find Jackson scribbling wildly on two sheets of paper.

At the top of each page, there was a title: "Reasons to Stay" and "Reasons to Go."

"What on earth are you doing?" I asked, wiping the sleep from swollen eyes.

"Making life easy for you." He looked up at me and smiled warmly, "You deserve a break!"

Then he handed me the two sheets of paper inscribed with lists of reasons. The "Stay" page had 8 bullet points while the "Go" page only had one.

Jackson sat back in his chair, staring at me as I read the lists.

At bullet point 8 on the "Stay" page I burst out laughing, "What's this? It read: "Stay and be my flat mate." I looked over at Jackson, one eyebrow raised as I contemplated his offer. Jackson blushed, stumbling his words as he recounted, "Well, you can probably tell I need some help with the bills! It's freezing in here. You stay – we turn the heat on."

I chuckled, "Well! That's an offer I simply can't refuse!" I rubbed my hands together. "But – are you sure?"

"Of course! Stay as long as you need! I could do with some company around here," he replied.

I immediately thought of Isabella and the other girls on the shop floor. *May as well give them something to talk about!*

"OK! But only if you are sure…I don't want to overstay my welcome or anything like that!"

"No worries. I'll let you know the moment you do," Jackson smiled as he tore up the "Go" sheet of paper.

14

KEEPING UP APPEARANCES

As Isabella battled a seemingly never-ending cycle of turgid morning sickness, I fought the never-ending desire to smack her in the face. I didn't know what was worse: the silent but sympathetically simpering looks from my co-workers or the constant discussions about cute baby names.

Have they no consideration for my feelings? Don't they think it's weird that she is having a baby with my husband?

At locking up time, I put my personal possessions away in my locker. I reapplied my red lipstick, taking extra care to fill in the lines before blotting with a tissue and reapplying a second time, then I quickly topped up my eyeliner with a deft flick of the wrist. My life may have been shattered across the four corners of the globe but there was no excuse for showing my despair in my appearance.

Making my way towards the staff entrance door, I stepped out onto the sidewalk and bumped face-first into Rick.

Fuck! What is he doing here?

"Willow!" he gasped, "How are you?"

His disheveled appearance took me by surprise. I thought back to the days when he would wait outside Devonshire Department Store in the freezing cold. There he would stand with his navy pea coat, collar pulled up high around the back of his neck, shielding himself from the harsh Scottish winter. His black wavy hair falling over one eye. Now, his appearance shocked me.

"How do you think I am?" I responded flatly, trying not to reveal any signs of lingering affection that I might still be harbouring for him. In his wavering hand, he clutched a brown envelope.

This can't be good.

Following my gaze, he handed the envelope to me.

"It's from Homeland Security. They've requested another meeting with us."

As if on cue, Jackson burst forth from the building, lit a cigarette, and stepped closer to me, eyeing Rick. He gave a curt nod.

"Looks like he's got a letter for me," I broached, inspecting the government stamped envelope, "I wonder how you're going to explain your *little situation* to them."

"Look, we don't even know if the baby is mine," Rick faltered, shifting his weight from one foot to the other. Acute discomfort written across his face. His eyes refusing to meet mine.

"Now you're attempting to deny you are the father?" I gasped, unsure of how exactly I had ever become entwined with this situation. Disgusted, I attempted to walk away as Rick made a desperate attempt to get Jackson to intervene.

Rick pulled Jackson by the arm, pleading with him.

"Jackson, you remember that night…the night I was due to fly off to Glasgow, don't you?"

"Oh, no way!" Jackson held up a hand, "You're not getting me involved in this." Jackson backed away from Rick.

"Bella and I had a huge fight, remember?" Rick's eyes were bulging, as he desperately willed Jackson to remember a distant event in the past.

I sensed Rick was clutching at straws.

Jackson looked at me like he wanted to make his escape as quickly as possible, but Rick was having none of it.

"I don't even remember what we were arguing about but then you called and asked Bella if she wanted to go clubbing, remember?" Rick pleaded, staring at Jackson intently, urging him to answer the question.

I sensed that Jackson knew exactly where this conversation was going.

I intervened and attempted to pull Jackson away from Rick, "Oh please!"

Rick became more desperate, "You remember that night, don't you Jackson?" I looked on as Jackson took a long drag on his cigarette as if to buy time while Rick continued to question him.

"You guys went out on the town and I went to the airport", he declared.

There was a lull of silence as Rick stared at Jackson and I.

"Don't you see?" he implored, "For Chrissakes, do the math! There is no way that baby is mine."

I wanted to believe him—I really, really did. The math made perfect sense, but I had made this mistake once before, with Finn. The guy, who in Geneviève's eyes, was too good for me. The same guy who went out and got another girl pregnant while he was going out with me.

It was that day, when he had made the announcement that he was going to be a dad and that he was leaving me, that I had installed my protective shield. That was the day I promised myself that no other man would hurt me the way he had just done. But here I was again, in the exact same position, only this time, I was on the other side of the Atlantic.

"And the reason I met you Willow, is because I went into your store to buy her a bottle of perfume – to make it up to her…and all this time it looks like she was cheating on me with someone else!" Desperation filled the air as the irony of his own words were completely lost on him.

***

I felt Rick attempt to place his palm in mine, shaking me out of my thoughts. It was hot, sweaty. I immediately pulled my hand out of his; he was not going to weasel his way back into my affections – no chance. Refusing to return his gaze, my body language instinctively took over. My stomach began to loll as a sickening feeling developed rapidly in the pit of my stomach.

"So, let me get this right…you were shopping for her in my store when you asked me out?"

Rick realized there and then it was over.

"So, you're not coming home with me?" he implored, eyes frantically searching mine.

Glancing at him fleetingly, I noticed sadness well up. It took all my strength to turn and walk away from him. The tinny tapping of Jackson's winkle pickers echoing in the background was the only sound I heard as I walked on alone.

15

SOLUTION

The next morning, as Jackson and I rode the subway to work, I wondered how many more times I would make this journey with him before I overstayed my welcome. He had been a darling about it all, but I was not going to impose upon our new friendship—he was, after all, the only real friend I had in this town.

As we embarked upon the business of the day, Mrs. G took up her usual spot in the middle of the beauty hall floor. I noticed she was clutching a batch of paperwork, nothing unusual about that I supposed, but there was something different about her, something I couldn't quite put my finger on.

"Ladies and Gentlemen, hush please," she commanded; in that all-encompassing authoritarian manner I had grown to respect. At least you knew where you stood with Mrs. G.

Mrs. G cleared her throat in preparation for her next sentence. At once, a wave of silence washed over the shop floor as workers came to a standstill. I waited anxiously as conversations around me came to a halt and I noticed that some of the women were holding hands.

Oh no! What's going on here? Everyone looks so worried.

Mrs. G wielded an air of authority over her staff. She knew she had us in the palm of her hands. I hoped she would be gentle with us.

"I have an important announcement to make," she stated, looking around the beauty hall while staring at us all individually, taking her time, before delivering her next sentence.

Uh oh, don't like the sound of this.

"Some of you may already be aware that D'Arcy's Department Store has been under considerable financial stress as of late. This unfortunate situation has been going on for quite some time."

Dammit, this is all I need!

Jackson gave me a "told you so" look while some of my co-workers looked like they might burst into tears at any moment. Then it struck me. I wasn't the only one who was struggling to get by. Those carefully applied masks that my co-workers wore worked hard to conceal what was going on underneath, but who knew what their home lives were like? We were all in this together.

"I have already taken steps to increase sales and you will have noticed by now that I have already moved my two top salespeople onto the Blake's Apothecary Counter."

This statement amazed me. I had no idea I was considered one of the top sellers. Looking over at Isabella, I wondered if this was one of the reasons she disliked me so much. Mrs. G shot me a warning look.

"And to improve sales still further, I have decided to launch a competition."

A wave of excitement washed over the women; some of whom clapped their hands in approval while a few of the more cynical types displayed a look of jaded disgust. Mrs. G immediately shot the little group of dissenters a warning look.

"The aim of the competition is to find out who is the best overall makeup artist in New York City. Each top department store will enter one of their makeup artists into the competition, here at D'Arcy's."

One of the dissenters, an older woman called Noreen, shook her head in disgust while others around her clapped and hollered their approval.

"Wait! There's more!" Mrs. G continued to stare through us, demanding our utmost attention, daring any of us to talk over her. "The winner of the competition will work on the Carlotta Rossellini Team of International makeup artistes at New York Fashion Week."

The mere mention of the name Carlotta Rossellini caused the women and Jackson to whoop and holler their approval, so much that even dull Noreen joined in.

"Hush, hush please…there's more."

The crowd became silent. A couple of the women embraced each other while others listened intently.

"Depending on requirements there may even be an opportunity to work at London Fashion Week with Carlotta's team."

The beauty hall floor workers erupted in excitement. Most of these women had never been out of the country, never mind go to work in London with one of the world's most prominent makeup artists.

Mrs. G allowed us to see a rare smile, as she clearly had us all in the palm of her hands.

"The press will be in store tomorrow evening to talk to some of you, so I'll need all hands on deck and absolutely no absences. Got that?"

I looked on enviously as some of the women hugged each other. I couldn't quite believe what I was hearing, and looking around at the others, I felt like an outsider looking in at a glamorous party that I was not invited to. Mrs. G sidled up beside me, catching me off guard, "The winner of the competition will also receive valuable status that will help with a Green Card application. I think they call it the Exceptional Ability class." Winking at me, I understood completely what she was trying to tell me, that winning this competition might be my only chance at staying in the country in my own right and making it on my own.

The sweet sensation of possibility ran through my mind. *Could I really stay here on my own, build a life all by myself—have my own status and not be dependent on anyone else—be the mistress of my own destiny?* There was only one thing for it, I would have to enter that competition and give it my all; see if I could achieve something important all by myself.

As soon as Mrs. G sidled off, Jackson whispered, "You should enter. It could be the answer to all your problems."

"What are you? A mind reader? But I'm guessing I don't stand a chance next to Isabella," I bleated, suddenly feeling sorry for myself, scolding myself for even thinking there might be a possibility.

"Hmm…I see your dilemma," Jackson completely understood where I was coming from.

The futility of anyone going up against Isabella was obvious. She was Art School educated and held a Masters in Fine Art. The queue for her Saturday afternoon makeovers sometimes went outside the building and down the street. It would be a total waste of time and energy putting myself up against her. Isabella was the Queen Bee of D'Arcy's Department Store Beauty Hall and everyone knew it. She and Carlotta Rossellini would make quite a team. My heart sank at the realisation. The stark truth was I had not a chance in hell of winning that competition.

***

Later that evening, after a visit to Lola's Bar, I felt tipsy on drink and high on possibility. Jackson had spent the whole time in the bar pontificating about ways in which I might win the competition while I drank, silently listening.

Back home with him, I kicked off my heels and hung up my coat while Jackson boiled the kettle.

"You want tea?" he shouted through the thin walls.

"Yes please, and a chocolate cookie… if you have any?"

There was no more satisfying way to take the edge off an alcohol-fueled night than with a mug of steaming hot tea and a chocolate biscuit to dip in it. As I walked back into the living room of Jackson's apartment, I could see he had already taken up prime position in his regal, sage green velvet winged armchair. He looked every inch the English lord of the manor, dressed head to toe in pristine black, crossing his long skinny jean-clad legs. I observed him as he sipped on his tea, secretly thanking the Lord above that he had put Jackson into my life.

"Be a darling and press the button on the answering machine?" he asked.

"Yes, m'laud," I quipped, pressing the button as I sat down on the couch to listen.

"Willow. It's me. Rick. I've... er...decided to do the right thing by Isabella and support her with the pregnancy. I'll send the rest of your stuff around tomorrow. Goodbye."

Sobering up in a flash, the chocolate biscuit fell out of my hand and splashed into the hot tea, scolding my leg. The burning sensation echoed the sense of panic building up inside me - as the full realisation of his short message hit me. Staring at Jackson, a well of tears built up, Jackson stared back, mute. Looking like he was trying to compute all the gigantic implications of that one short message. My one and only chance of staying in the country had now been swiftly taken from me. Without Rick in the equation, and with no hope in hell of winning the Makeup Artistry Competition, I would have to return home – a failure.

"Willow, calm down, will you? No matter how bad this situation is, we can sort it. We'll find a way. I promise you." Jackson took control and stood up.

"Don't tell me to calm down. Don't you see? He's just gone and taken away the only chance I have to stay here," I bleated, tears brimming, ready to spill down my cheeks.

Jackson looked at me, crestfallen. The penny had finally dropped.

"There's got to be a way!" Jackson started pacing. "You can't go back. Not now. Not after everything you've been through!"

He was right. There had to be a way.

16

EARL GREY AND CUCUMBER SANDWICHES

Jackson and I arrived at D'Arcy's ten minutes earlier than usual. It had been a sleepless night for me, fraught with tossing and turning, unable to find a soft spot on the hard couch or the solace I was searching for. I had listened all night long for the sound of the alarm, telling me it was now time to get up and get on with the day. When the alarm finally went off, I felt an instant sense of relief that the day was beginning. My brain had been whirring the whole night long trying to find a solution to the position I now found myself in.

We set to work on the Blake's Apothecary Counter, unpacking boxes and making up little gift bags to give to our clients. Jackson had already pre-ordered chintzy teacups from homewares on the third floor and one by one he had handed them to me, indicating for me to give them a quick rinse in the beauty hall sink.

Every so often, I would catch Mrs. G loitering a second or two longer than was necessary at our counter, keeping a careful eye on proceedings. She was such a stickler for detail. All she had to do was raise one eyebrow to silently communicate that something was awry on the counter. Following her gaze, I would instantly know which pile of wonky cups she was alluding too. This woman did not miss a trick. When everything appeared to be to her liking, she would nod silently then move on to the next counter. D'Arcy's Department

Store would not be D'Arcy's without Mrs. G at the helm, that was for sure. Funnily enough, although formidable to the outsider, the longer I got to work alongside her, the more I came to admire her.

As soon as Mrs. G walked away from our counter, I heard Jackson mumble under his breath.

"What is it?" I asked.

"Don't turn around...Bella's on her way over."

"Shit!"

It was the moment I had been dreading, the moment of Isabella's victory lap. The moment when she would take great enjoyment in getting her own back.

Stay strong. Stay calm. You can do this. Don't give yourself a showing up on the shop floor.

Taking a deep breath, I stood up to full height, drew my stomach in, placed my hands on my hips and summoned the inner strength to stare back at Isabella. To my surprise, Isabella didn't say anything, instead, she just stared back, almost willing me to speak first. A look of malice lay behind that perfectly painted face; beauty really was skin deep. I sensed the other workers had noticed Isabella approach our counter, and one by one, they appeared to stop their activities on the shop floor. The situation reminded me of a John Wayne film, where two cowboys would approach each other slowly, sussing each other out, before brandishing their guns.

Just then, Isabella lurched forward, placed her arms over her tiny baby bump, groaned, and then smiled straight at me.

The baby had just kicked her.

I felt sick to my stomach. I took a few steps towards her, keeping my gaze on her at all times.

"You got what you wanted. Now get the hell away from me," I demanded, slightly shocked at the power in my voice.

Just then, one of Isabella's regular customers stepped in between us.

"It's three o'clock. I have to pick the kids up shortly. When are you going to start my makeover?"

Isabella scowled at me then drew daggers at her customer.

"Go and take a seat. I'll be over in a minute," she indicated.

The customer looked at me then at Isabella before deciding it would be better to leave at once.

"I'm over this. Cancel my appointment. Jane at Macy's can do it instead," then the woman rushed off.

Isabella made her way across the shop floor to my counter. She held a thick white embossed envelope in her hand.

"This is for you," she stated.

Confused, I took the envelope from her and opened it, while Isabella looked on, smiling.

I read the words on the card and felt instantly like I had just been punched in the stomach.

"Rick and I have picked out a gift list at the Baby Registry in Saks Fifth Avenue."

Then she turned on her heels and walked away.

I hate you.

Mrs. G saw everything and strutted over to Isabella.

"Have you just lost a customer?" she asked, eyebrow raised in indignation. "See me in my office at the end of the shift." Then she turned to face me, "Willow, haven't you got work to do?" Her expression speaking a thousand words.

"Yes, Mrs. G."

One by one, the other women returned to their duties, while a few looked over at me with faux sympathetic expressions. I walked over to the trash bin located near Isabella's counter and threw the white envelope in. I'm sure she saw me.

I turned to face Mrs. G who was determined to carry on with the important business of the day, Mrs. G announced, "Willow, Jackson, I've arranged for the press to come in tonight, just before closing. They're going to take photos of the both of you working behind the counter."

This was a shock to me.

Newspapers? Me in the press? Whatever next?

"Oh, and just to give you the heads up, they might want to interview you, so be prepared for that to happen."

Interview us? Why would anyone want to interview us?

Mrs. G stepped closer to the counter, making sure to keep her voice down low, she continued "I'll need you both to change into fresh uniforms about an hour before they arrive. Got that? I want everything to be perfect."

I smiled inwardly at the prospect of my name in headlights in one of the city's leading newspapers, but Jackson appeared to be unmoved and distinctly unimpressed by the whole thing.

"Which newspaper is it?" he asked.

"New York Times – lifestyle section," Mrs. G responded coolly, although I could sense a ripple of excitement was burgeoning under that icy exterior.

Suppose there is no such thing as bad press when you have a struggling shop.

Jackson shrugged his shoulders dolefully. His reaction confused me.

The New York freakin' Times? Shouldn't he be excited?

I figured out that maybe all this publicity stuff was just not something that Jackson was interested in...

To each their own, I suppose.

I set about the tasks at hand before being distracted by a pleasantly plump looking woman in her late 40s. She wore an old-fashioned paisley print dress which clung to her in all the wrong places.

Strutting straight into salesperson mode, I motioned for the woman to take a seat.

"Madam, would you care to sit down?"

The woman smiled inquisitively as she shifted her heft onto the barstool, panting breathlessly. I stood and watched as she struggled to get onto the leather stool. Finally catching her breath, she took the cup and saucer from me and blurted out, "You from England," and without waiting for an answer she slurped the tea, "I love the English accent, makes you guys sound so intelligent. Are you clever, honey?"

Smiling from ear to ear, I couldn't help but like the countrified ways of this woman. I didn't have the inclination to explain to her that I was Scottish, not English, and I found her to be a refreshing antidote to some of the regulars who graced the beauty hall floor. Jackson and I exchanged knowing looks but neither of us wanted to burst her bubble.

"I'd like to think I was, but I'm sure others would disagree!" I replied, smiling warmly.

The woman looked at me with a blank expression, she hadn't understood a word of what I had just said.

I shrugged.

May as well be speaking bloody Japanese at this rate.

Jackson smirked. His cut-glass accent was much easier for Americans to understand.

Maybe I just need to slow down a bit and pronounce my words better, I thought.

"What's this you're giving me?" The woman stared into her cup of Earl Grey tea, "I ain't never seen the likes of this before."

"It's all part of the service. Welcome to Blake's Apothecary. Now, how can I help you?"

"I just came in to buy a mascara," she answered, gazing up at me all the while, "But now I think I'll take a look at this lavender and honeysuckle skincare collection you have here." The woman paused to scrutinise the contents of the gift box. "What do you recommend for me?" she enquired. I analysed her skin through her makeup, examining the texture of her skin and how the makeup sat in the lines and ridges that had formed on her approximately 48-year-old face. I recommended she start using a nourishing serum followed by a deeply replenishing Shea butter and honey moisturizer.

Analysis over, I had the woman eating out of the palm of my hand.

An hour into our shift, we were clearly running rings around the other counters as customers flocked to learn all about our variety of organic skincare and makeup. Perhaps it was the simple pleasure of drinking tea while having their makeup done that swung it in our favour. Whatever it was, our normally cosmopolitan, cocktail-loving clientele seemed to be enjoying the fragrant taste of Earl Grey infused with lemon, complemented by a seemingly never-ending supply of delicate cucumber sandwiches freshly prepared by D'Arcy's canteen kitchen. With the crusts cut off – of course!

As the clock ticked relentlessly onwards, we made sale after sale, working in tandem: one of us cashing up and capturing our customer details, while the other continued with makeovers, hand massages, and effusive compliments. At one point during the afternoon, it got so busy that Mrs. G had to bring in foot soldiers from some of the quieter counters, much to the chagrin of the other beauty floor employees. No one, not even Mrs. G, could possibly have anticipated how wildly successful our counter would become. The day was made even more enjoyable by the sight of Isabella kicking off her platform shoes as she ran off to be sick in the staff toilets, three times in the space of an hour.

As I watched her bolt off for the fifth time that afternoon, I couldn't help but smile inwardly. I was only human after all. After her seventh trip to the bathroom, I felt a tad sorry for her. Then I pulled myself to task – *how could it be that I felt sorry for the woman who was supposedly carrying my husband's baby? How could that be?* Sometimes I wasn't able to decipher my own thoughts. Everything just seemed so crazy and mixed up. I thought back to the times when I had visualised myself as a new mother. I had the vague idea I might be quite good at it, but I suppose deep down, a small part of me was afraid that I might not be up to par.

Hours passed, but the melee at our counter showed no signs of slowing, much to Mrs. G's pleasure. From time to time, I would grab a moment to look up from my makeovers and only then did I notice the aggrieved expressions of my colleagues. We were the only counter making serious money, and it was not going down too well with the others. But no matter how much money we brought in, Mrs. G could be seen out of the corner of my eye, staring at me, unnerving me, watching our every move. At one point, I noticed her catch my attention then she stared at my underarm area. Following her gaze, I blushed with embarrassment when I noticed pit stains had become visible.

Shit!

Still, there was no time to worry about what anyone else was thinking, I had my own situation to think about. No matter which way I looked at it, there was no clear-cut solution to any of it.

A quote from the yellow book flitted into my mind as I packaged up a $300 sale:

When you don't know what to do, the best course of action is to do nothing.

As the afternoon turned into early evening, and after clocking up sale-by-sale, I finally took a moment to look up from the cash register. Jackson had been gone on a break and had finally made a reappearance. Leaning over, I angrily whispered in his ear, "Where the hell have you been all afternoon? I'm sweating like a pig." Jackson gave me one of his classic 'Really?' looks, causing me to pause for a second. Indignantly, I handed him my customer's purchases, "Take these. I need to go get changed before they get here."

Jackson shot me a warning look as he half-heartedly tallied up the purchase on the till, "Oh no! You're not leaving me—no way!"

"What? What do you mean? You've been gone for the best part of the last two hours. I've got to go get changed. You afraid of getting your photo taken or something?" Then I bolted before he had time to answer.

Inside the relative peace and quiet of the staff toilets, I examined the creeping pit stains brought on by almost five hours of non-stop sales and exertion on the counter. Mrs. G had already silently indicated what was going on in my armpit region, but I hadn't been able to do anything about it until Jackson returned. Now, I had exactly five minutes to get ready before the press arrived. I quickly reapplied my favourite Ruby Woo by MAC and fixed my hair into a smooth gleaming bob just as Mrs. G made her presence known.

"Ahem," she interrupted. "You do know they've arrived? Don't you?"

Mrs. G scanned me from tip to toe as she always did when she spoke, "Jackson is holding court for the moment, but I want you to go out there and really woo them. Do your best. Talk up a storm about working at D'Arcy's."

"Certainly!" I replied. "Will do."

At that moment, as I changed into my fresh black uniform dress, I realised I wasn't the only woman in the room who was trying to keep it all together. Mrs. G's steely vice-like grip on D'Arcy's was floundering in front of me. Who knew what pressure she was under to stay afloat? An unspoken camaraderie began to develop between us. I was like a delicate seedling battered in a winter storm and Mrs. G was the protective blanket of snow, sheltering and urging me to grow, perhaps hoping that she too would somehow benefit from my success. Her words cut like shards of glass into my thoughts, "I want you to tell them about the Makeup Artistry Competition and how, if you win it, it might help you to gain citizenship and stay in the country. You do know that, don't you?" she asked before giving me the time of day to answer.

Her presence literally took my breath away. She had given me my first chance to prove myself and now she was offering me another. I decided then and there that I owed it to this woman, and to myself, to do my absolute best. If I was going to be in with even the slightest chance of winning, I would need to. But deep down inside, I pondered how I could go up against Isabella and win. I just didn't see how it could be possible.

Mrs. G left and the staff toilets were empty once more. I took a twirl in front of the full-length mirror, pulled my shoulders back and inhaled deeply before stepping out into the bright lights of the beauty hall just as Ella Fitzgerald belted out the opening notes of "Sleigh Ride."

Giddy up giddy up... our cheeks are nice and rosy…we're snuggled up together…

I made my way through the throng of customers, towards our counter. An air of excitement drenched customers and staff alike. The aroma of fresh pine needles was being pumped out into the store, while twinkling lights on the throngs of Christmas trees placed all around the store danced in time to the music.

Who could not love the run-up to Christmas in New York City?

17

ONCE BITTEN

I strode confidently in Jackson's direction. I could see him being interviewed by a smartly dressed female journalist, but there was something about his stance which struck me as strange. *Why does he look so sullen?*

The journalist, a skinny woman around the same age as myself, closed her notebook, "I think I've got everything I need," she snapped matter-of-factly, indicating that the interview was over.

She removed her black-rimmed glasses and placed them on top of her head. I saw her signal to her photographer to pack up his belongings.

Wait! What about me?

As I caught up to the counter, Jackson looked me up and down, then drew me the dirtiest look he could possibly muster. I was at a loss.

What the fuck is going on? What about ***my*** *interview?*

The photographer, a thin, spiky looking man with a sharp chin, gruffly moved out of my way, striking my elbow with his equipment in the process.

"Ouch, watch where you're going, will you?" I shrilled in his ear, attempting to make myself heard over the store sound system.

Giddy up, Giddy up…Ella Fitzgerald continued to bellow out.

Ignoring me, the photographer summoned his colleague to his side, "Let's get us the hell out of here." Dismayed by his rudeness, I couldn't believe my ears when he shouted to the journalist, "We've still to report on that new launch at Macy's, maybe they'll offer us something a little more interesting than this crap." Then the photographer leaned in and muttered something incomprehensible in Jackson's direction, before making his way out of the store.

Then he was off, making his way towards the journalist who was standing outside in the rain, guarding his equipment and staring at her watch. I turned and stared at Jackson.

"What a foul man! Would you mind telling me what the hell is going on? I didn't even get a chance to speak to them." Placing my hands on my hips, I continued to chastise Jackson, "Mrs. G will be furious with me when she finds out."

It was the first time I had ever lost my temper with Jackson, but I appeared to be having no effect on him whatsoever.

"Haven't you got anything to say?" I demanded an answer, desperate now as Mrs. G inched her way through the crowd towards me. Jackson continued to ignore me. Instead, he concentrated hard on packing up his own belongings in preparation for making his exit.

"Remember I told you about the man I fell in love with? The one that brought me over here, then dumped me three weeks later?"

"Yes, I do." *Uh-oh!*

Jackson looked over at the weasel man on the sidewalk.

"That's who he left me for."

Shocked, I burst out laughing. I couldn't help myself.

"No way! Him? What a horrible person! Why would anyone choose him over you?"

These words were music to his ears. Jackson's mood appeared to brighten slightly.

So, this is why he didn't want the press coming in from that newspaper.

"Sorry, you never got the chance to talk about the competition. I gave the reporter all the details. They're gonna cover the story over the weekend."

"They are?" I paused. "Well. That's fantastic," I exclaimed, delighted for both myself and Mrs. G.

I still had no clue how I could possibly go up against Isabella and win, but I had to try, at least.

Later that evening, as we arrived at Jackson's apartment door, we were shocked to see Rick standing waiting on us. Jackson remained silent as he let himself in.

"You go on...I'll be in in a minute," I said as I turned to look at Rick.

"Hello, Willow."

Rick stood at the side of Jackson's apartment door, staring at me.

Shit.

The familiar rolling and swelling erupted in my stomach.

Keep it together, keep it together.

I felt my face redden as I stared back at him. He shuffled from one foot to the other, looking as nervous as hell.

"I brought you your stuff…I thought you might be needing it."

I could smell the familiar scent of cedar wood and vetiver. It was his favourite fragrance, I had bought it for him from the Duty-Free at Glasgow Airport just prior to departing for our brand-new life in New York.

Keep it together. Keep it together. Stay strong girl.

Rick handed me an overstuffed bag of clothes that I had forgotten to pack that fateful day, the day I had decided to leave him. It all seemed so long ago now; so much had happened since.

I placed the bag by my feet, not exactly sure of how to proceed. Rick immediately took control of the situation, wrapping his arms tightly around my waist, pulling me close to him. My heart sped up as we stared at each other. His eyes searched mine as my heart raced.

"Can we start again?" he asked, a huge smile creasing across his face, as hope-filled his eyes.

There it was – the question I had been dreading. Yet, a part of me had wanted him to ask.

Stay strong Willow. You can do this.

I averted my gaze.

Sensing that I was pulling away from him, Rick continued with his PR campaign.

"You know you still love me. C'mon Willow…be honest…you and I can make this work."

Why did he have to go and make this so difficult?

"I don't think so, Rick." I responded civilly, trying my best to sound like I really meant it.

That's it! Stay strong girl. Don't let him sucker you in again.

"What do you mean, you don't think so? For Christ's sake Willow, they're not exactly queuing up in droves to invite you out, are they?"

The bloody cheek of him! Who the hell does he think he is?

"The whole Isabella thing is just one big mistake…we don't need to let her ruin what we've got going on…think about it at least, will ya?"

That name sent a shiver down my spine.

"I have thought about it Rick and the answer is still no."

I stepped away from him and turned my back to him. All I could think of was getting inside Jackson's apartment and closing the door on him.

Rick's painful attempt at consoling me descended into desperation as he attempted to block my entry into the apartment.

"I mean, you'll be needing ***me*** if you want to stay in the country."

There it was. I could feel the blood boiling in my veins.

"I need YOU?" I shouted, kicking his foot away from the door jamb, "Are you for real?"

Grabbing my belongings and my keys, I opened Jackson's door on my second attempt and went to slam the door shut, but Rick had once again placed his foot between the door jamb preventing me from shutting it tight. In the narrow gap that separated us, any residual feelings I had for him turned to ice as we stared at each other. Rick was aghast at my response. Things were clearly not going his way, causing him to use the only weapon he had left.

"But…but they'll kick you out if you don't come back to me!"

I stared in utter disbelief at the man I had fallen head over heels in love with.

"Then let them!"

Closing the door on him, I heard my voice say defiantly, "I no longer care."

But Rick wasn't finished yet. He pushed the door open once more,

"So, you won't be attending tomorrow morning's meeting?" he asked.

I turned to face him, confused.

"What are you talking about?" I asked.

"The Green Card interview…they brought it forward to tomorrow morning, but I'm guessing you won't be attending…" Rick turned away as he prepared to leave.

"Wait! Hold on…what time is it at?"

"10:00 am. 37 Nassau Street."

I weighed up my chances.

We could still pull this off. It was worth a try at least, I thought.

'Ok. I'll be there." I said matter of factly, assuming control. "Make sure you are on time."

18

CAMOUFLAGE

I arrived ten minutes early for our Marriage-Based Green Card Fraud Interview, hoping to make a good impression and get there before Rick turned up. But when I arrived, he was already positioned on a chair, pretending to look at a government-supplied magazine while I made attempts at polite interaction.

I could tell he was feeling as nervous as hell.

"Hi. How are you?" I asked, peering into his eyes but he wouldn't look at me.

Shit, Willow. You're going to have to try harder than that.

"Be like that. No need to be so bloody rude," I pressed, hoping for some kind of reaction.

Finally, Rick looked up at me despondently. He stared into my eyes but said nothing. I couldn't believe it had come to this. *Where was the spark we once had? Where had the passion gone*? Inside I felt as hard as concrete like my core was made of iron girders. I knew that in order to stay in the country, I was going to have to ace this interview.

A thin, tall man in his late 40s walked into the waiting room to greet us. He carried a thick file under his arm, and I noticed large sweat stains around his armpits. He seemed nervous which did nothing to allay my own anxiety.

What's he got to be bloody nervous about? I thought.

"Mr. and Mrs. Delgado? Pleased to meet you both. My name is Mr. Hendricks. I will be conducting the interview this morning…please come with me."

His expression was strained as he invited us both into his lair.

"Take a seat," he invited.

He indicated for us both to sit opposite him at the pristine desk.

"We'll go over a few details, then you'll be interviewed separately. The goal today is that both sets of answers are almost identical to each other," he remonstrated.

My stomach swelled with anxiety as Rick nudged my foot with his scuffed boot. I refused to look at him.

The next five minutes consisted of a set of easy questions about our current address, when we arrived in New York, and our current employment. I knew that the next set would not be so easy to answer.

"Mrs. Delgado, would you come with me please?"

I looked up at the officer then turned to face Rick. He avoided my stare.

"Of course," I replied. *Where's he taking me?*

But even I knew my attempt at forced politeness was wasted on the three of us. Clearly, no-one was in the mood. All three of us just wanted this over and done with.

The kindly officer took me into a small, airless, windowless interview room. The austere grey paintwork had been vandalised by previous interviewees, and the officer was clearly embarrassed about his poor working conditions. He caught my eye, then lowered his gaze and blushed slightly, "I do apologise for the surroundings, they keep telling us our office space will be upgraded but it never seems to happen. Anyways, let's get back to the task in hand. I will be recording the interview. Please take your time with the answers and Mrs. Delgado…"

"What?" I asked, feeling somewhat shaken out of the sense of comfort that he had tried so hard to establish.

"If you don't know the answer, please say so…there is to be no guess-work. Got that?"

Is he on to me? Does he know something I don't know?

The nerves ricocheted through me, causing me to cough unexpectedly.

""S'cuse me. The air is so dry in here."

"Let me fetch you some water," he offered, getting up out of his seat.

He looked like a man who hated every minute of his job.

"No. You're quite alright. I'm fine really. Just feeling a little nervous that's all."

The officer placed his hand over mine, patting my hand, unnerving me with his closeness. It was like he had invaded my personal space and I didn't like it one bit.

"You've absolutely nothing to be nervous about." He stared right through me, "Now, shall we begin?"

I nodded my head in agreement.

I'm hardly going to say "no," am I?

The next hour played out, as if in slow motion. The officer pressed the record button on his old-fashioned tape recorder, then indicated for me to start answering the questions.

"Mrs. Campbell-Delgado, please can you tell us your neighbourhood garbage pickup days?"

Crikey, I have no bloody clue. That's not my department. I clean toilets. I don't do garbage...

"How the hell should I know? It's not my job to put out the garbage. I clean the toilets; he does the bins!"

The officer looked at me with a droll expression then carried on with the next question. I composed myself in my chair, pulling my dress down over my knees and began fidgeting with the cuffs of my coat.

Inside, part of me was angry for having to go through this stupid situation in the first place while another part of me wanted to do my level best. I was conflicted, torn in half. I was resentful yet strangely compliant.

"What colour are the curtains in your accommodation?"

Shit! What colour does Rick have?

Then it came to me in an instant, "We have no curtains, just blinds." The officer ticked off a box on his sheet of paper and wiped sweat beads from his forehead. The questions appeared to be benign.

What's his problem? These are easy, I thought. *He's making a big deal out of nothing!*

"You're doing fine Mrs. Campbell-Delgado, now tell me what each of you eat for breakfast?"

Easy peasy!

"I'm a night owl so I don't eat breakfast. Neither does Rick but sometimes he'll grab something on the run…just depends really."

Bingo! Aced that one!

The officer looked up from his paperwork and looked straight at me once again. His eyes glinted with mirth, "How many remote controls are there in your home?"

I exhaled in relief. This was like being on a quiz show. I was even beginning to loosen up and enjoy myself.

"Just one. We're always arguing over it. He was a bachelor before he met me."

Liar, liar pants on fire.

"Does your spouse listen to the radio? If so, which station?"

"He's hooked on The Archers. BBC, I think? I introduced him to it when we first met in Glasgow. He thinks the posh English accents are hilarious."

The man smiled back.

This is going better than I thought. Got him in the palm of my bleeding hand, haven't I?

"Is there a particular food that you eat each week? If so, what is it?"

"Chicken Chow Mein!" I stated confidently.

I hated that dish, but it was all I could think of to say. Rick and I hadn't known each other long enough to establish a favourite weekly dish.

The officer looked up from his notes and smiled at me.

You go, Willow!

"What is your favourite restaurant?" He went on, his voice taking a slightly more serious tone.

Beaming with confidence, and thoroughly relaxed, I regaled the officer with my next answer, "Now that Sir, is impossible to answer…I mean how the hell you expect me to have a favourite restaurant in New York when I've only been here like two minutes?"

"Point taken. Let's move onto the next question, shall we?" he indicated, seemingly in a hurry to get everything over with.

The officer looked closely at his notes, face blushing flame red. He cleared his throat, half apologising as I gripped onto the side of my chair in anticipation.

"I apologise in advance but I have to ask you some personal questions now…I hope you understand."

Crikey Moses, I don't like the sound of this… What can it be?

The air of confidence I had acquired disappeared like a puff of smoke in the wind

"What kind of birth control do you use? What brand do you use?" the man kept his eyes firmly on his paperwork as he spoke. I almost felt sorry for him.

"Oh…I see…erm, I'm on birth control. The pill."

The officer's face reddened further, as he scribbled notes on his paper.

"I really do apologise for the next question."

"Go on then," I urged, dreading the words that would come out of his mouth.

"What is your favourite position? Cowgirl? Doggy? Missionary?"

Now this question explains the pit stains on this poor man's shirt! Yikes! I can't even remember the last time we did "it!."

"Am I allowed to use the Fifth Amendment on that one?" I asked cheekily trying my best to inject a dose of humour into the proceedings.

"Well, number one, you are not American so no, you can't use it, and secondly, I need an answer from you," his tone was changing with me now. It was clear he wanted this over and done with just as much as me.

Wonder how much he gets paid for making people squirm in their chair? OK, get serious Willow. Think back to the wedding night…no don't think of that, that was the night I discovered the lipstick in the bathroom. Go back to the rented apartment on Ingram Street. What did we do there?

"I really can't allow you much more time to answer the question Mrs. Delgado," he looked at his watch then at me, "It's beginning to appear like you don't know the answer."

OK! Here's hoping for the best.

"I hate to sound boring, but let's put the missionary position down for that one."

"Will do," he replied, flicking the paper over to the next set of questions.

Now I was sweating, and I needed to pee. The officer had expertly lulled me into a false sense of security with the easy questions and now they were getting more and more difficult to answer. I was sure he could see the cracks in my veneer. He wasn't as innocent as he was making himself out to be.

"What time did you wake up this morning?" he went on, this time looking me straight in the eyes.

Shit! What the hell am I going to say to this one?

I fidgeted once more with the coat cuffs and crossed and re-crossed my legs, hoping to put some pressure on my bladder so that I didn't pee myself.

"You must know the answer to that one surely?" I could tell he was beginning to lose patience with me.

Blurting out the only answer I could come up with, I said, "I work shifts, so I don't have a regular wake up time."

You must do better than that, Willow.

The officer stared harshly at me, serving to heighten my anxiety levels sky high

"Let's just say it was around 7:30 am," I went on, trying my best to stay in control of the situation.

The officer scribbled more notes then looked at his watch. I could feel the interview slipping away from me. Then he hit me with the final nail in the coffin, "Did you come to the interview together? Who drove?"

Aw no!!! What am I going to say to this one?

I was convinced the officer could see trickles of sweat running down my forehead, as my knuckles whitened.

Why hadn't we prepared for this interview. Why didn't we bring a lawyer with us?

"Mrs. Delgado, could you please answer the question?"

Resigned, I exhaled the answer, "We arrived separately."

The officer gave me a knowing look then spoke into the tape machine.

"Interview terminated 11:35am on Tuesday 10th December 2019."

"You said what?" I couldn't quite believe my ears. I had been released from the interview room 20 minutes before Rick was let go, and from his stance alone, I knew instinctively that things had gone awry for him too.

Rick stirred his spoon around and around in his coffee cup, refusing to look at me. He exuded an air of nonchalance and arrogance from his every pore. It was easy to see now from his answers how little he really knew me or even cared for me. He had made no attempt to answer the officer in the correct manner. In fact, as I sat there getting angrier and angrier with him, the little voice in my head told me just to give up.

He had told the officer that I did have a favourite restaurant, that my favourite position was cowgirl (*in his dreams!*), and that we always fought over the three remotes in his apartment. Oh, and he mentioned to his interviewer that he did have curtains, ones that Isabella had installed the day of my departure, supposedly to mark her territory now that I was gone.

Disgusted, I stood up and moved away from him, making my way towards the exit.

"I'm going," I stated.

"Wait! Where are you going?"

"Home."

19

EMPIRE STATE OF MIND

The run-up to Christmas is always an exciting time in retail. The hard-sell of new launches is suddenly replaced by throngs of mostly men queuing up to purchase luxuriously wrapped gift packages for their loved ones. The prettier the box, the more impressive the price tag and they were like putty in the palm of our experienced hands.

It wasn't unusual to hear, "Give me three of those" or "I'll take five as long as you wrap!"

It was also the time of year that could make or break department stores. They needed robust sales in order to survive the rest of the year.

Then there was Mrs. G, frantically trying out every trick in the book. Trying to stay afloat and prevent the family's long-standing wealth from disappearing down the drain.

Who would want that kind of responsibility on their shoulders? To be the generation that wiped out a fortune built up over centuries. I had to hand it to Mrs. G, she appeared as cold as ice like butter wouldn't melt in her mouth. But underneath, I guessed she was just the same as the rest of us. We were all trying to survive in this concrete jungle called New York.

After a particularly grueling day on the beauty hall floor, dealing with irate customers who were unhappy that their skin hadn't cleared up the way it said it would on the packaging, it was a relief to grab a seat on the subway. I went over and over a conversation I had earlier with one of my regular customers who had experienced a breakout in her skin. She had brought the half-used product back and had demanded a full refund. It happened all the time. It was a case of choose your battles.

As I played the conversation over and over in my head, I noticed that Jackson appeared lost in thought.

"What's up with you?" I asked.

"Oh…nothing much…just got a favour to ask…" he mumbled as if to himself.

"Ok. Go on!" I encouraged.

Jackson turned his face towards me, his expression appeared slightly troubled.

"When we get back to the apartment…do you mind leaving for a while?"

"Why...What's going on?" I enquired.

"I've got a date," Jackson blushed slightly, shifting in his seat uncomfortably. "Charles from accounts is coming over for dinner at 8."

"Well! Look at you!" I joked, feeling faintly hollow inside. "Going on a hot date!"

"Yeah! Who would've thought it? This will be my first date since…well, you know who."

"Aw, you'll be fine" I encouraged, "Charlie is a lovely man."

Inside, I was screaming. *No! He's not! He's a man-eater! A horror! And it's Saturday night—where am I supposed to go, alone???*

Jackson must have read my thoughts.

"They're playing Devil Wears Prada at the Roxy. I hope you don't mind but I bought you a ticket."

Hold on!

"You did?" I asked. "I've seen it five times already but …oh well, never mind."

We arrived at our stop. Both of us deep in thought. As soon as we entered the apartment, I strung into gear. It was a pleasure to be able to help out Jackson, after everything he had done for me.

"You get the hoover and I'll clean the dishes.... have you got ingredients for the dinner?" I asked. Jackson looked at me.

"Well, you better run down to the store and get some. Have you any idea what you are going to cook?"

"Pasta?" he suggested half-heartedly.

"Look, you go and get a shower and I'll nip down to Mario's and get stuff for a Thai chicken curry, he'll like that, won't he?" I asked.

Secretly, I imagined how unbearably hot I could make it then thought better of it. Charlie had never been particularly pleasant to me whenever I enquired about my late paycheque but I'm guessing he was in deep trying to keep D'Arcy's afloat.

Half an hour later, the apartment was filled with the aroma of lemongrass, coconut, and fragrant Thai sauce. I had cleaned up the dishes and gave the bathroom a quick spritz. I then replaced Jackson's scruffy towel with my treasured pristine white Donna Karan towel set. Afterwards, I lit a small tea candle and placed it in one of Jackson's empty votive holders. I turned the dimmer switch down low to create a more ambient effect in the apartment and finally, cranked up the thermostat. I fluffed the cushions then slammed then with the side of my hand, in a vain attempt to give the five-star hotel effect. It wasn't working. All that was left to do was roll up my bedding and hide it somewhere, but where? The apartment was tiny with very little in the way of closet space. I decided to cram the duvet and blankets into the hall closet where we kept our winter coats and boots. It was already filled to capacity but just then Jackson appeared from his bedroom and helped me push the duvet in. Then he slammed the door shut and looked at me.

"Well? What's the verdict?" he asked, "How do I look?"

His appearance took my breath away. His long black silky hair hung over one eye and he was dressed head to toe in black. He had applied black eyeliner and painted his nails neon blue.

"Not too shabby!" I stumbled. *You go Jackson!*

It was as if I was seeing him for the first time as my memory flitted back to him introducing himself to me in D'Arcy's, that fateful morning I went out looking to buy a kettle.

Jackson appeared uncharacteristically self-conscious.

"Is it too much?" he asked.

"No! Not at all!" I replied, hoping that my facial expression matched my voice.

"Thanks for cooking the dinner and cleaning up the apartment. The place looks great and it smells great too!" Then he looked over at the sofa at the line of cushions all standing to attention, "But what is that all about?" he laughed.

I noticed the time on the living room clock. It was 7:50pm.

"I better make my escape then," I suggested. "Three's a crowd…n'all that."

I hadn't had time to do anything about my own appearance. I was still in my work clothes and my makeup needed a touch-up. My signature red lipstick had all but disappeared except for a faint pencil line around the outline of my lips. Not a good look for someone who works in the industry, but oh well, Jackson was my priority.

Walking me to the door, he smiled, "I really appreciate this, Willow…oh and don't forget this," he handed me the cinema ticket. I noticed the screening was scheduled for 9:00pm.

"You be good…and if you can't be good…be careful," I heard myself say.

For fuck sake Willow, what are you saying? Get out the apartment and leave him alone!

***

I walked along the crowded pavement making way for the groups of friends and loved up couples heading out for an evening of revelry in the bars and restaurants of Queens. I walked past our favourite dive bar, unable to summon up the courage to walk in alone. Instead, I decided to kill twenty minutes in a tiny Italian café. I ordered an espresso and slice of millionaire's cake and thought back to Jackson, who would now be having dinner with Charlie…or maybe they had moved on to other activities…I brushed the thought aside as I devoured the thick layer of chocolate. In the background, Alicia Keys could be heard singing "Empire State of Mind." I had never paid much attention to the lyrics, but now it felt as if she was talking straight at me.

I smiled wryly to myself as Alicia described the city I had now come to think of as home. But as much as I loved the song, it caused me an aching sadness that I might not be able to stay and make all my dreams come true. The fear of having to return to my past was never far away. It was the sole fear that propelled me on.

I gulped down the last residue of thick black coffee and pulled on my coat, buckling the belt tightly around my waist. The film was starting in 10 minutes. I had never been to the cinema alone. It wasn't something I had ever thought about doing. If there was a film I really wanted to see, there was always someone willing to tag along. Squeezing into my seat, I initially thought myself lucky to be sitting alone, then I looked all around me. It was quite clearly date night. I was the only singleton surrounded by a sea of smooching couples.

Christ almighty. I shuddered as I slunk down into my seat, trying my best to look inconspicuous. It was just me, Andrea Sachs, Miranda Priestley, Emily, and Nigel for the next hour or two. About an hour into my favourite movie, I noticed the couple in front of me were starting to get rather amorous with each other. As much as I attempted to avert my gaze, there was something about the man's silhouette in the darkness that piqued my interest. I accidentally on purpose dropped my unopened bag of crisps on the floor so that I would have to bend down and pick it up, as I did, the unmistakable scent of vetiver and cedar infiltrated my nostrils.

No! It can't be! Oh my God! But the woman…who is she? I pondered to myself as I sat back in my chair studying the back of Rick's head.

Whoever she is, she isn't Isabella. Strangely, I felt bad for Isabella, sitting at home …

Feeling sick to my stomach, I couldn't sit there any longer. I had to leave. I bundled up my belongings and made my way along the aisle, stepping on toes in my rush to get out of there.

"Ouch! Watch where you're going, idiot!" one young man shouted as his eyes bulged in pain.

"Sorry, so sorry," I whispered as I bundled myself out of there. I prayed to God he hadn't seen me.

I couldn't wait to make my escape out on to the busy street. It was a relief to sidle into anonymity. It was raining heavily, suiting my bad mood perfectly.

I can't even go to a freakin film without bumping into him…

I checked the time. It was 10pm. I couldn't stay out any longer. I needed to get home and go to sleep. It had been a long day and I was tired.

I put on my headphones and listened to Simply Red's "Holding Back the Years." The singer's lament perfectly echoing the way I felt.

On arrival at Jackson's apartment, I put the key in the lock and held my breath as I anticipated the scene behind the door. I coughed loudly, alerting the habitants to my presence, then opened the hallway closet door only to be met with a hastily unravelling duvet falling on top of me.

"Aargh! I forgot I put that in there!"

"You alright?" Jackson called.

"Yeah. I'm fine… Where's Charlie?" I asked looking around for signs of his presence.

Jackson wore a hang-dog expression. "It didn't go too well…" he grimaced. "Turns out he's vegan and allergic to lemongrass…. oh!" Jackson smiled. "And me!"

I tried to suppress a giggle.

Really? This is the funniest thing I've heard all day!

"What do you mean he's allergic to you?" I asked, a stray look of glee threatening to erupt across my face.

"Well…I went in for a snog and then he started sneezing," Jackson shrugged. "He wouldn't bloody stop." He waved his hands. "Enough about me, how did **you** get on?"

"Awful! Just awful!" I replied haughtily, throwing myself onto the couch, secretly glad that Charlie had left.

"But I thought it was one of your favourite films?"

"It was… is…just wasn't impressed with the audience," I silently indicated to Jackson who I was talking about.

He got it straight away.

"No? They weren't there…surely not," he shook his head.

"*He* was," I responded. "With another woman."

"What?" Jackson asked.

He shook his head in disgust, "He's never gonna change…was like that all the way through college, thought he would have grown out of it by now, but apparently not…"

"What do you mean? College?" I asked.

"Didn't he tell you? That's how we met…he was over in London on a year abroad and we landed up in the same business class. The ballet school made us take business class as a back- up. Rick had some family ties to the school…et voila! We were buddies from the get-go," he explained, "We stayed in contact after that."

"He never told me any of that. Never once mentioned it to me. Bloody man of mystery," I said sadly.

I could tell Jackson felt bad for me, "I feel such a fool, Jackson."

Jackson leaned in for a hug.

"So, your night has been just as shit as mine?"

"Yep," I responded.

"What a pair we are, eh?" Jackson declared.

I stood up and went into the kitchen and shouted through, "You want tea and a chocolate cookie?" There was no answer. Jackson had left the apartment. He had mumbled something about going to buy a newspaper.

Confused, I stirred the milk into the mug. As I settled into the couch, pulling the blanket over me, I sipped the tea and replayed the night's events in my head. Twenty minutes later, Jackson made a re-appearance. In his hands, he held a rolled-up copy of the New York Times.

"Thanks for helping me out tonight love, I'm turning in to read the paper. Night night," he said. "Oh, and don't wake me… I'm on a late shift."

"Ok. Night Jackson. I'll see you at 2:00 tomorrow."

***

Early the next morning, as the wind battered noisily against the double-glazed window, I threw on my black uniform dress, packed a small lunch bag with a bottle of water and a microwavable lasagna for lunch, then tip-toed quietly alone out of the apartment; as Jackson was working a later shift, there was no reason to wake him. Apartment secured, I glanced at my watch, and marched on.

A sea of downcast faces greeted me as I arrived at D'Arcy's staff entrance. I made straight for the locker room, shaking the icy particles off my winter coat and slipping out of my flat biker knee-high boots. They had been one of my better purchases during my stay in New York. Perhaps subconsciously, I had bought them knowing that they would do double duty in Glasgow too. Placing the still wet boots in the locker, I glanced at my reflection and smoothed my hair into its usual neat black bob. I avoided staring too deeply at my own reflection.

As I walked on to the Beauty Hall floor, there was a sense of something in the ether as my colleagues huddled tightly, looking towards the door to Mrs. G's office.

A stream of uniformed officers was entering and leaving the office, carrying out boxes of files, while Mrs. G remained inside, barely visible through the open door.

I looked on, shocked.

"What's going on?" I asked Jake.

"D'Arcy's is under investigation...Homeland Security is here. They've got Mrs. G in the office. She looks a mess...feel so sorry for her."

"Oh my God! This is awful."

"They could close the whole store down in an instant...if they want to," he said.

I felt bad. Real bad.

Is this somehow my fault?

Activity on the shop floor continued as Cecil opened the doors to a throng of customers who wanted to get in out of the cold.

We all banded together and got on with our jobs, serving customers and pretending as if everything was normal while officers continued to search Mrs. G's office. There was no sign of her. But then a strange thing began happening, on the shop floor. One by one, employees were taken into Mrs. G's office for questioning, only to be escorted off the premises by an armed guard a short time later.

I decided to work through my lunch hour. The employee count on the shop floor was diminishing rapidly. At 1:45pm, I saw Jackson walk through the public entrance to D'Arcy's.

That's strange. Why is he not using the staff entrance?

He was wearing a heavy three-quarter pea coat with the collar turned up and wore a flat cap with the skip pulled down over one eye. He made his way directly towards Blake's Apothecary, his complexion ruddy from the cold easterly wind blowing outside.

He stood in front of my counter wearing a determined expression as he watched the officers' conduct their investigation.

I recognized Officer Jamieson in the throng of customers; he was making his way towards my counter.

Shit!

"You're early," I said. "You're not on duty till 2:00pm."

Jackson adopted an aloof expression as he clocked eyes with Officer Jamieson.

"Sorry, don't know what you are talking about," he responded, "can you let me try the L'eau Hiver please?"

What the fuck? What is he doing? What's going on?

I looked intently at Jackson. Silently questioning him. He stared back keeping his gaze higher than the top of my head.

Why is he acting so strange?

Mr. Jamieson stood at the side of my counter, watching on intently…saying nothing.

I turned around and took the tester of L'eau Hiver off the glass shelf and silently handed it to Jackson. He stood coolly in front of me. Sprayed some of the perfume on the slim sheet of cardboard, wafted it in the air, all the while not taking his eyes off me. I noticed a bead of sweat make a trail down his right cheek.

"How much is it?" he asked in his cut-glass English accent.

I played along. "95 dollars," I replied. "Would you like a bottle? We currently have it on promotion. You get a gift bag. Makes an ideal Christmas present…" I trailed on, my words slowing as my heart began to break. I realized Jackson was saying goodbye to me.

"Yes. I'll take it," he responded, staring intently at me like he was silently communicating.

The voice inside my head screamed, *"Don't blow his cover."* I painstakingly wrapped the perfume, and swiped his credit card, my hand shaking as Shirley Bassey belted out "Big Spender." I recalled the long conversation we had a while back about being "escape artists" in New York.

Everything began to fall into place.

I handed the distinctive D'Arcy's gift bag over, my fingers grazing Jackson's hand, a second or two longer than necessary. He smiled at me as he left last night's newspaper rolled up on the top of my glass counter. Then he was gone. Out of there and out of my life. I wondered if I would ever see him again.

Mr. Jamieson looked at me. I stared back at him.

"What?" I asked, exasperated.

"Nothing." Then he turned and walked back towards my boss's office.

I felt like I might throw up.

20

PANSTICK & SPACKLE

The shift ended unremarkably as I completed my handover with Rose, who had been transferred onto my counter from Designer Shoes mid-afternoon. I had always thought Mrs. G was a fast worker but this time she had really surpassed my expectations. As she was being led out the store by Homeland Security officers, she barked orders at the remaining staff on the shop floor. Rose was a gift. She was highly trained, pleasant and easy to get on with. She could work her way around a set of makeup brushes like she had been practicing her whole life for this very moment. During the day, she had quietly revealed to me that she was heartsick of smelly feet and had longed to be moved to our department since her first shift in the store. I had to hand it to her, if I'd had to work with feet all day long, I wouldn't have lasted half as long.

"Now you know how to cash up the till, don't you?" I asked, hoping against all hope that I would hear the correct answer.

Rose was studying Architecture at The Spitzer School of Architecture and hoped one day to practice in Europe, but for now, she was solely concerned with the detailed packaging on The Daisy Chain Lipstick Collection.

"Of course, I do. Now don't worry about a thing. I'll be just fine," she uttered, urging me to get on and leave her alone. As I entered the staff changing room, the scene shocked me. Rows upon rows of metal lockers with the doors having been prised open to reveal the personal belongings of staff who would likely never return to D'Arcy's Department Store. An eerie sensation chilled my spine as I shuddered. Jackson's locker had also been prised open.

I rushed all the way back to the apartment, stomach rolling, hoping and praying that Jackson would be there, sitting in his winged armchair, drinking his tea, like some regal lord of the manor. Instead, I entered the cold dark apartment and instantly knew I was alone. There was no sign of him. He had packed up the few belongings he owned and left. Left me alone in his apartment.

I threw myself down on the couch, holding my head in my hands.

"What do I do now?" I asked myself. Out of the corner of my eye, I saw the yellow book lying on the coffee table. "This is all your fault," I thought. "Wish I had never bloody read you. Would never be in this mess."

I went into the kitchen and switched on the kettle, as I waited on it reaching boiling point, I hugged myself, deep in thought. Just then, a white D'Arcy's bag caught my eye. Inside lay the unopened bottle of perfume that Jackson had purchased earlier. It had a little note attached.

'For you, Willow, love Jackson. P.S. Rent is paid till end of month…wish I could have paid more.'

So, it really was true. Jackson was gone. The photographer had outed D'Arcy's Department Store and Jackson in the New York Times article on illegal aliens and now he was on the run from the police. I began to cry as I realized that I might never see him again. Huge belting sobs erupted out of me. My emotions shocking me to the core.

21

THE NEXT STEP

Early the next morning, I struggled to get out of the makeshift bed I had made up on the couch. I couldn't bear the thought of sleeping in Jackson's bed. I couldn't help but feel sad for him as I envisioned how life must have been for him for the past seven years. But I had to admire him too. Opening the door to his bedroom, I peeked in, feeling somewhat disrespectful.

He certainly had me fooled. Then it struck me. The training. The ballet training he undertook as a young boy. *He must have picked it up at ballet school in London.* All the little pieces of the puzzle were beginning to fall into place. Jackson had managed to expertly pull the wool over everyone's eyes. Wherever he was right now, I could only imagine how low he must be feeling. I thought back to that fateful night when the newspaper reporter and photographer had come into D'Arcy's. I remember feeling confused by Jackson's lack of interest in the whole thing. Now, I could see he must have been dreading his secret being exposed – *that photographer! The nasty little man!*

***

The morning shift flew swiftly by, as it did every day at D'Arcy's. I attempted a smile as I noticed an endless stream of women making their way straight towards the newly launched limited edition L'eau du Buttercup – a fine mist spray infused with the scent of buttercups. The fragrance lit up the atmosphere like kindling in a roaring grate on Christmas Eve. But my heart was just not in it.

Blake's Apothecary had only dispatched two cartons of this magical stuff but already there were 42 names on the waitlist. Now standing in front of me was customer 43 – an elegantly dressed woman in her mid-40s who wanted to buy a bottle to send to her cousin in Nebraska. I half-heartedly took down the woman's details, as Lucinda, one of the perfume girls who worked part-time on the Nars counter, whispered in my ear, "Did you hear the good news?" I tried to signal to her that I was with a customer, but she was having none of it.

Turning my attention back to my counter, I carried on as if she was invisible.

"Thanks, Mrs Jones, I'll call you as soon as the L'eau du Buttercup comes back in stock."

Lucinda was poking me in the ribs as I spoke, causing me to squeak in a high-pitched voice. Mrs. Jones gave me a strange look but continued on her way.

Turning around to face my colleague, I mocked her, "Good news? Didn't think there was such a thing?"

Refusing to register the cold breeze blowing between us, Lucinda continued, "Isabella and Rick split up last night." She looked at me intently as I continued to write Mrs. Jones's name on the client waitlist. My belly rolled and swelled as I strained to maintain my composure. She went on, "She's staying with me till she gets her shit together."

On hearing the "s" word, Mrs. Jones turned around to face Lucinda, drawing her a dirty look, not quite believing she had the nerve to use such a trashy word on the shop floor.

"Oh? I'm very sad to hear that," I replied, while not allowing myself to feel anything.

I noticed Mrs. Jones linger awhile, a little too eager to find out more. I decided to put her out of her misery.

"You see Mrs. Jones, my husband who I married in Scotland and moved to New York to be with, decided to go back and live with his ex and dump me on the assumption that he is the father to his ex's child."

Lucinda turned to walk away but then stopped and whispered, "Turns out the baby is not his after all."

22

CHRISTMAS IN NEW YORK

It had always been a long-held dream of mine to spend Christmas in New York. Years of watching ice skaters fall and laugh on TV as they sped around the ice rink in Central Park had led me to believe that you hadn't truly lived until you had done this. With limited funds and no friends to speak of, I was determined to make my dream come true.

On foot, I set out on the Sunday morning two days before Christmas and made my way through the throng of tourists and locals, towards the Central Park. Although the horse-drawn carts looked like a more inviting way to get around, I decided to leave that activity to the lovebirds.

On I went. Determined to bathe in the absolute romance of my surroundings. I pulled the woolen scarf up high around my nose and ears and pulled my hat down as far south as it would go, leaving only the cross-section of my eyes and ridge of nose visible. The icy air bit at me, causing me to shiver and catch my breath. When it got to the point of freezer burn hitting my forehead, I decided it wise to turn back and head for the warmth of the subway and Jackson's apartment. I had two days before his tenancy agreement would run out and the placard inviting me to leave the premises would be placed on the front of his door – for all to see. Two days and still no plan of action. In entering the apartment once more, I made myself a mug of hot tea and settled down into Jackson's winged armchair. I wondered what might become of this chair – his most prized possession. In fact, I wondered what might become of the remainder of Jackson's possessions: his bed with the super-soft brushed cotton bed sheets and duvet cover, his collection of shoeboxes which appeared to contain a smattering of personal belonging accumulated over the years, and then, there were his small but select collection of cooking appliances. His three copper pots and Le Creuset cast iron grill. I knew Jackson had dropped some serious cash on his cookware, but I had no idea what to do with any of it. Taking the mug of tea with me, I went into the closet and pulled out my black Kate Spade clutch that contained a bunch of dollar bills that I had managed to save up. Unfortunately for me, they hadn't miraculously multiplied their contents. I counted the dollar bills and came to the same figure I had the last time I counted the money. $625 and five cents.

I sensed a wave of despair was about to overwhelm me at any minute.

What the freakin hell am I going to do?

I had already searched the classifieds over and over and it was more than clear that $625 would only get me a box room in a shared dive in one of the more insalubrious sides of town, worse still I would still need to find a deposit. That's if I were to stay. That same $625 was also the *price of a cheap one-way ticket home.*

Where's my yellow book?

I threw myself down on the couch and switched on the TV. Audrey Hepburn was sitting on a windowsill in a New York apartment not dissimilar to the one I found myself in. She was singing "Moon River," looking effortlessly gorgeous and elegant while I was feeling fat and frumpy under all those layers and, if I were perfectly honest, feeling like a bit of a fool.

I dipped the last remaining chocolate biscuit into my tea and thought of my mum. If she were alive, what would she tell me to do? I wondered.

I heard her silently echo into my subconscious…*Go home darling, go home.* I knew she was around me, all the time, silently guiding me and supporting me as I flew in the face of one disastrous situation to another. If only it were that easy. If only I had someplace I could really call "home."

I opened the yellow book at a random page. It said, "*Are you standing in your own way? Let your creative gifts shine.*"

What creative gifts do I possess?

I thought long and hard but nothing much came to the surface. Then it struck me like a bolt. My creative gifts are working with makeup. It's the run-up to Christmas. Girls need pampering before a big night out. Why didn't I think of this before? If I could drum up enough business, I might be able to earn some extra cash to tide me over and at least pay another month's payment on the rent. Buy me some time.

I opened Jackson's old laptop and set about designing myself a little flyer:

New Year, New You Makeovers by Willow

Only $65.

Book now and reserve your spot. Will travel to your home or place of work.

Then I forwarded my document to an online printer and ordered my first batch of 100 flyers. I would have to speculate to accumulate but there was no time like the present to get working on my little side hustle.

Exactly two days later, I was placing the flyers in strategic spots around the staff room and canteen, drumming up business. Rose had helped spread the word with her former colleagues in Shoes and George in Gadgets had promised to do his best by me. I think he had a soft spot for my Scottish accent. Whatever it was, he was willing to help me out.

By 5pm, I had precisely 8 bookings lined up with the last one booked for New Year's Eve. 8X65=$520. Almost enough to pay rent for the next month. I knew that this practice was frowned upon by most department stores but as Mrs. G was otherwise occupied by her own troubles and she knew the inner workings of my complicated life, I suspected that she would turn a blind eye to my entrepreneurial ways. I was right.

Later that evening as I prepared to leave for my first appointment with Sheila, one of the canteen cooks, I was handed an official letter from Deborah in HR.

Oh no! Don't like the look of this!

The familiarity of the thickness of the letter brought memories surging back from the fateful night in Devonshire's, when Greta had handed me a thick white envelope. The envelope held a written warning. One more strike and I would have been out of a job if I hadn't made the monumental decision to change the direction my life had been going in.

Deborah wouldn't make eye contact with me.

What is this? Last one in the job, first one out of a job?

I opened the envelope there and then, scanning the contents while searching for the three words that would seal my fate. There they were, expertly hidden between the HR speak and hyperbole: *"Terms of Redundancy."*

D'Arcy's Department Store would be closing at the end of February and I was being given two months' notice. Deborah had already moved on to her next target. My redundancy offer was minimal. One months' extra pay and a reference. I couldn't complain really. I was only just in the door and I was lucky to be offered anything. I did the mental math and deducted that I could survive till March. Breathing a sigh of relief and thanking the angels for granting me this stay-of-execution, I smiled at Deborah and went on my merry way. At least now I could relax and enjoy the remainder of my extra time in New York while I figured out what to do next.

***

Flying by the seat of my pants might have become second nature to me but not so for the other employees, many of whom were wandering about in a state-of-shock. A few of the women had only known D'Arcy's as their employer since leaving school. I understood the shock waves they were currently feeling. I, on the other hand, had been walking around the store with an invisible shield of armour around me, making me invincible to what was going around me. I wondered if there might be something wrong with me, but then it dawned on me. After everything I had been through in my lifetime, I had grown with each grueling challenge. I was a changed person. I felt like I was *indefatigable*, that nothing could permeate the armour I wore. This inner well of strength shocked and frightened me a little.

"Willow, I'm assuming you have received your letter?" Mrs. G enquired, searching my eyes. I wondered what kind of inner hell she was going through right now, to be losing her life's work. Her hopes and dreams about to be flushed down the pan. The bail money alone had amounted to $300,000, a sum of money that had been rustled up by selling every stock and share she had amassed over the years.

"Yes. I have it."

I didn't know what else to say.

"I have recommended you to the Beauty Hall Manager in Macy's. She is happy to interview you, that's if you decide you want to stay?"

she enquired.

"That's very kind of you. Thanks for thinking of me."

"No problem. I would only recommend you if I thought you were up to the job. I have my reputation to think of, you know."

Reputation! Reputation! Oh My God! She will never work another day in this city. The authorities will make sure of that.

I felt heartbroken for Mrs. G. It was as if she was still holding onto whatever thread of hope she could muster. She was facing very serious charges and possibly looking at jail time.

"Thanks for offering me a job, Mrs. Gerson." I felt the tears well up. I could see that my boss' armour was on the verge of melting. We shook hands and parted ways. I ran all the way to the staff toilets, gripping on to the white porcelain sink as I burst into tears. I realised that I wasn't as strong as I thought I was. The tears that fell were testament to that. Pulling myself together, I dabbed my makeup and thanked my lucky stars it was a Kat von D day and my foundation was intact. I made a mental note to fill up my sample pot the next time I went past that counter.

***

On my return home to Jackson's apartment, I made payment on the rent. There was no need for the concierge man to know that he had left the building.

***

It was only five days till Christmas yet the gloom that hung over the store was palpable. Mrs. G had already told us she was planning on having a huge closing down sale but not until after the Makeup Artistry competition. It made perfect sense.

Word was beginning to get around D'Arcy's clientele and they were not happy. The store had been a catalyst in many of their lives. It was the place where they went to buy outfits to celebrate major events in their lives: from baptisms and christenings to communions and proms. There was even a small bridal pop-up that sold lingerie and silky accessories for the big day. Many of the staff were like close family friends to the customers. Repeat business was a huge part of the weekly takings but depending on where you stood on the political spectrum, feelings on immigration ran high. It was estimated that Mrs. G's employee numbers dropped by a third, the morning of the big reveal in the newspaper. Many workers just never showed up again.

There was also a huge question mark hanging over my name as I was in the middle of a complicated immigration application of my own. My meeting with Homeland Security was a disaster and it was only a matter of time before they summoned me.

Why does life have to be so bloody complicated?

Nevertheless, I chose to enjoy this time in my life as much as was feasibly possible despite the set of unusual circumstances I found myself in.

On Christmas Eve, as Mrs. G closed the store and most of the workers had rushed off to be with their families, I guessed she wanted to talk to me about something. I was right.

"Willow…are you in a rush?"

It was the moment I had been dreading, one that had been put off for far too long, the moment that both Mrs. G and I had been skirting around, the moment she would ask me about Jackson.

"Come with me, let's grab a glass of bubbly and relax for a bit, eh?"

Mrs. G indicated for me to follow her to a little corner of the shop floor that had been turned into a welcoming living room area complete with winged armchairs situated at either side of a fake Georgian fireplace. The fireplace mantel had been festooned in fairy lights, and Christmas garlands while the atmosphere hung heavy with the pungent smell of cinnamon and orange. On a tall round table lay a silver platter of sandwiches and a bottle of champagne chilling nicely in an ice bucket, accompanied by two crystal glasses. I smiled inwardly at the absolute awkwardness of the scenario, but there was nothing else for it to but to sit down and wait on the slew of unwelcome questions.

Mrs. G wore a weary smile. She looked physically exhausted.

"I'm not going to ask you about Jackson. I wouldn't put you in that situation…all I want to know…is he OK?"

I had no idea where Jackson was, but I thought it best not to worry Mrs. G.

"Yes. He's perfectly fine. Quite comfortable I would say!"

Enough now, Willow! No need to go overboard.

I reached forward and clinked my glass with hers and smiled.

"He's doing fine. You know Jackson. He's a survivor. He's been through a lot worse than this. He'll get by."

I didn't quite believe my own words, but I wanted to somehow reassure the woman who had been looking out for him all these years.

"Are you sure?" she asked, searching my face for clues.

"Absolutely, he's going to be just fine…you'll see."

I knew she wanted to ask me more, so much more. But we both knew it would be wise not to. Who knows, the store may have been bugged by the authorities. Mrs. G knew inwardly she would have to do with just the tiniest morsel of information. I looked on as she sat back in her seat and exhaled.

I wondered how long she has been dying to ask me about him.

"Now, what about you? What's going to happen to our little Scottish makeup girl?"

I felt embarrassed that the spotlight was now firmly on me. I hated attention of that sort. I wasn't used to anyone being interested in anything I had to say. It had been that way for so long now I just accepted it.

"Me? Oh—I'll be fine."

The familiar rolling and swelling sensation in my stomach erupted into a wave.

I had absolutely no clue whatsoever what was going to become of me.

My boss placed her glass down on the side table and stared at me, directly. Unnerving me. I froze.

"Is there any future for you and Rick?" she asked.

Now that's bordering on the personal, I thought. I wondered what she already knew about the situation I was in.

"I only ask as I'd love for you to be able to stay..." Mrs. G pressed her lips together and her voice trailed off. We sat in silence.

I knew what she was really thinking. That I had no hope in hell of winning the competition and being able to stay legally, under my own name.

There was a burning question whirring away in my brain, something that I desperately needed to ask Mrs. G, yet was scared. Then out of the blue, I heard myself blurt, "Why did you help the likes of Jackson and me? I mean, it would've have been easier to just get on with your own life...you know, running your own business..." I immediately regretted asking.

Mrs. G stiffened for a few seconds while she thought of her response to my question, then she softened, took a sip of her champagne and settled back into the armchair, all the while holding my gaze.

"You know, Willow, this country is built on immigration. There would be no United States of America if there were no immigrants. We should be proud of our immigration heritage, proud of a country that opens its arms to all who want to better themselves and make a good life for themselves." Mrs. G took another sip and swallowed. "I wanted to give you both an opportunity. My own name "Gerson" is Hungarian. It means "stranger" or "the banished." My family came here in the 1940s; they settled in the Queens area and have stayed ever since. I am carrying on the family tradition, living up to my name it seems, helping the strangers and the banished."

Freakin hell! This woman is something else!

I sat back and smiled at my boss, taking in all she had just told me. Visualising her family arriving from Hungary, destitute and homeless, dependent on the charity of strangers. I remembered how she had taken me in and twinned me with Jackson. It all made perfect sense now. She was proud of me; she knew all about my strife and struggles and now she was facing a monumental one of her own. Her family had built up the department store and now, under her guardianship, they were going to lose it. Her losses were going to be far more reaching and gut-wrenching than anything I could imagine.

Now, it was Mrs. G's turn to change the subject.

"It's Christmas Eve and look at us!" she smacked the arm of her chair. "We should be getting home and getting settled for the night. Big day tomorrow!"

We both stood up and made to leave.

We were after all the mistresses of disguise, the masters of the art of concealing or revealing. It was what we did for a living and we were both rather good at it.

"Oops! I almost forgot this!"

Mrs. G leaned down the side of her winged armchair and picked up a small gift-wrapped package. She looked at me, then handed the gift to me.

"Merry Christmas, Willow! Now, don't open it till tomorrow!" she warned, knowing full well that this would be the only present I would be opening on Christmas morning.

"Happy Christmas Mrs. G...But you shouldn't have!" I replied, secretly delighted that she had bothered to get me something.

"I'm sorry...I don't have anything for you." I felt ashamed that I hadn't even thought of getting her a gift.

"You already gave me a gift – the day you walked into my store," she shrugged, "I have enjoyed every minute watching you grow into a fine young artist.

"Merry Christmas, Willow!"

"Happy Christmas, Mrs. G!"

***

Early the next morning, I awoke to my very first New York Christmas. The apartment was as cold as ice, but I climbed into an old sleeping bag and sat for most of the morning drinking mugs of hot tea while watching an endless run of festive season movies. My spirits were high considering my circumstances. I refused to feel blue at such an amazing time of year. I promised myself I would go for a walk to Central Park later in the afternoon, then I remembered the small gift wrapped in silver foil and tied with a white ribbon.

That woman has such exquisite taste.

I wondered what could be inside as I delicately unraveled the ribbon, enjoying every moment of anticipation.

Foil discarded, my present was inside an elegant white box, the kind you would receive on purchasing an expensive piece of jewelry. Slowly, I lifted the lid while perusing the contents of the box. I must admit, I was slightly disappointed to see that the only things in the box was a bronze key with a crumpled cardboard tag attached to some string.

What the hell is this?

I took the weighty key out of the box and read the address on the label:

24a West Park Avenue.

Why is she giving me a key to a property on West Park Avenue?

I searched inside the box for any further remnants of information, but the box was empty. There was nothing else for it. I was going to have to get up, get dressed and go and find this address. My heart raced with anticipation as my brain whirred. I racked my memory to our previous conversations, but I couldn't for the life of me remember my boss ever talking about this address.

I looked out of the window of Jackson's apartment; it was blustery, and I could tell it must be freezing just by watching the passers-by on the street below. I didn't even know if New York transportation ran on Christmas Day. There was nothing else for it but to pull on my warmest layers and head out the door on my very own magical Christmas mystery tour.

Forty-five minutes later I stood in front of a stunning lime stoned building that seemed to go up and up and up. This was unlike any other building I had been inside since arriving in the city and yet I held in my palm the key to apartment 24a.

The only problem now was that a doorman stood between me and access to the building.

"Merry Christmas, ma'am," he gestured, awaiting a response.

"Happy Christmas, sir," I replied, wondering what to do next.

"Can I be of assistance?" he enquired.

Then I was at a loss at how to play this thing out. Should I tell him that I have a key to an apartment, or should I just swagger in, pretending that I knew where I was going?

Think on your feet, Willow…say something!

"Yes! Perhaps you can help me. Gigi Gerson sent me. I have to pick up some belongings for her."

The doorman stepped aside and indicated for me to come in.

"Then welcome! Let me know if I can be of any assistance. Here's my card. Call down if you need me."

I accepted the card then made my way for the lift. The gilded lift whizzed me all the way up to apartment 24a on the 16th floor. As I stepped out into the hushed hallway and onto the plush carpeting, the memory of arriving at Rick's apartment flooded me, filling me with instant despair.

Not now…I am not going to feel like this when I am standing amid such luxury.

I shoved the memory away into a dark recess while I traipsed down the hallway looking for the apartment.

There's 18a, 20a, 24a must be down here somewhere…

On arrival at the door, I put the key in the keyhole and with bated breath opened the door. The apartment was in darkness, with only a night light illuminating the light switch. I flicked the switch on and stood back and gasped as the whole expanse of the apartment in front of me was flooded with light. Light of all kind illuminated expensive pieces of furniture.

"Hello! Is there anyone in?" I called in a low voice.

Silence.

Tentatively, I stepped in and closed the door behind me.

The open plan living room was minimally decorated but had enough sofas and armchairs to seat at least eight people. In the corner, a demurely decorated Christmas tree twinkled as the aroma of fresh pine hit my nostrils.

A real tree! Such class!

There were four rooms leading off the vast open plan living room: each one led into elegantly dressed bedrooms and each bedroom appeared to have its own ensuite bathroom. I recalled Rick describing his ensuite as "luxury as standard" but his ensuite was a broom cupboard in comparison. I realised then that he didn't have a clue what he was talking about…this is real luxury…quiet luxury.

Understated, yet sumptuous.

In one of the guest bedrooms lay a brown carrier bag with an expensive designer name inscribed on the outside. Inside the bag was a package wrapped in layers and layers of fine white tissue paper. As I unraveled the layers, I took out a pair of striped candy pink pj's. These were just not any old pj's. They were made from the softest brushed cotton and felt baby soft to the touch. I looked at the label. I still didn't recognise the Italian name inscribed on the label. As I pulled the pj's out for closer inspection, a small white card fell out and landed at my feet. It read:

For You Willow! I hope you are enjoying your stay in my apartment over the Christmas Holidays. Happy Christmas from Gigi Gerson!

Be sure to look in the fridge!

(I'll be home on the 26th)

I climbed into the pajamas. No one had ever shown me such kindness. I was gob-smacked but deliriously happy. I walked into the kitchen wearing my new pink pajamas and felt the underfloor heating warming my feet. At that moment in time, life could not have been more perfect.

I still had no clue as to why I had a key to this apartment. Feeling parched, I opened the huge refrigerator to look for a bottle of sparkling water. I knew how much Mrs. G adored her daily artisan water consumption and, lo and behold, there were six blue glass bottles on the top rack of the fridge, next to a yellow ceramic bowl of organic unwaxed lemons. On the bottom rack of the fridge lay a foil-wrapped cooked turkey. Stepping in closer, I could see there was a label in front of the bird which stated: *Reheat at 180 degrees for 45 minutes.*

Wow! Did Mrs. G really leave this for me? Did she want me to have a proper Christmas dinner? I investigated further. Inside the thermostat-controlled wine refrigerator was a single bottle of Chateau Neuf du Pape with a label around its neck: *To be drunk slowly and carefully.*

I smiled at the humour.

In one of the kitchen cupboards I found a traditional Christmas cake, with the instructions on how to cook, clearly labelled.

This woman thinks of everything! Oh well, better get to work.

I took the turkey out of the fridge and placed in in the centre of the oven, then opened the bottle of wine and poured myself a large goblet.

"Happy Christmas Willow!" I said aloud, to no one in particular.

As the smell of the turkey began to leak out from the oven and the soft glow of red wine had left its mark on me, I realised I needed to pee. Real bad.

It took a moment or two to find the main bathroom that was not conjoined with a bedroom. As I washed my hands, I looked intently at my reflection in the mirror.

Look at you girl! I mean holy fuck! If only they could see you now, washing your hands in your boss' fancy condo apartment on Park Avenue.

Grabbing my half-full goblet of wine, I sat down carefully on the cream leather sofa, making sure not to spill a drop. She would kill me if I did. I found the switch for the giant flatscreen TV and switched it on. More Christmas movies only this time I was not freezing my ass off in a crummy Queen's apartment. Then it struck me. Jackson!

What is he doing right now? Where is he? I wish he was with me.

My heart plunged as I thought of him holed up somewhere. If only he could be here with me now, lapping up such luxury. Life would be just perfect.

Ping!

The oven timer indicated that my turkey was ready. I reached in and carefully extracted it without spilling a drop of juice onto the spotless stone-tiled kitchen floor. I lay it aside and let it cool for ten minutes while I sipped on another glass of the wine. Mrs. G sure knew how to make a girl feel at home.

Feeling slightly tipsy, I dug into my Christmas dinner with much aplomb. The hearty meat satisfied an ache in my stomach that had been there for too long. Endless pot noodles and cup-a-soups had not been enough to keep me nourished and now my system was in shock. This felt like the first proper meal I had eaten in ages. The only upside to my monetary situation was that I was losing weight fast and furiously. My clothes were hanging off me but there was no spare cash to buy new ones.

After dinner, I carefully put the dirty dishes and glasses in the dishwasher and turned the TV off. My mood sank slightly as a semblance of hushed silence descended over the apartment. I switched off most of the living room lights, leaving but one lamp on, then lay back on the butter-soft leather and admired the cityscape view through the floor to ceiling windows. Through the windows, I could see small groups of people going about their business on Christmas night. I thought briefly about Geneviève back in Glasgow and considered whether to call her. I decided against it. I wanted to revel in this delicious solitude for as long as possible before having to face the gritty realities that tomorrow would bring. I pulled a cashmere blanket over me and rubbed my toes together as I gently drifted off. The warmth, the wine, and the luxe surroundings transpired to grant me one of the soundest sleeps I ever had.

Early the next morning, I was awakened by brilliant rays of kia-orange sunshine beaming through the windows of the apartment. Looking at the time on the iPad, I could see it had just gone past 6:00am. I reached over and closed the blinds before padding into one of the spare bedrooms. The queen bed looked more inviting than the sofa. I reset the alarm clock for 9:00am then snuggled under the down duvet and drifted back to sleep. An extra three hours sleep would set me up for the challenges of the day ahead.

23

HEAVEN OR LAS VEGAS

On my arrival back at Jackson's apartment, I received exactly what I expected. A note on the door front declaring in bold black letters that subject to section B1 of the tenancy agreement, non-payment of rent resulted in an end to the tenancy agreement. The locks had been changed and I was now officially homeless. I about turned and walked back out of the building. I had tried my best to summon up the money. I really had. But to no avail. I was now wearing all the clothes I had in my possession. My Kate Spade bag held a purse with a bunch of dollars, a small makeup bag, some notepads and pencils, and my passport.

As I stepped out of the shelter of the apartment lobby into the street, the wind cut through me like a scalpel through flesh. I had no Plan B.

I traipsed the streets for twenty minutes until I could stand the bitter temperature no more. Ducking into Lola's, I took a pew at the bar, in the place that Jackson and I had regularly frequented and ordered a coffee, the strongest type available. Taking out my purse, while being careful not to reveal it to passersby, I carefully counted the bunch of twenties over and over. Each time I counted; I came to the same number - $620. No more and no less. I fired up the iPad and checked the price of a one-way ticket to London on British Airways. There was a seat available on this evening's flight. If I booked the ticket, my dream of staying in New York would be over, that much would be true.

Just then, the music system in the drum belted out a familiar beat that stopped me in my tracks. It was the intro to "Empire State of Mind" by Alicia Keys. I took a sip of the hot coffee and let the lyrics wash over me. It felt as if Alicia was talking directly at me. I put my purse away, left a dollar bill for the barman, then stepped out once more onto the pavement where I expertly hailed a cab.

"Empire State Building, please."

The remainder of the day passed in a blur of plans. I wrote notes in my notepad as I stood at the top of the iconic building drinking in the views. I thought of the immigrants who had landed ashore at Ellis Island in the second half of the 19th century and the 20th-century engineers, architects, and welders who had built these towering skyscrapers with nothing but brute strength, determination, and adversity for bedfellows. Their circumstances would have been much harsher than mine to deal with. I had my health. I had my talent. I had buckets loads of determination, and like Alicia, I had a bucket load of dreams.

Surely I can make this happen? Surely I can do this?

For inspiration, I opened the yellow book and read chapter after chapter. I had read these chapters many times before, but now on this day, as I faced homelessness, each word was carved in my mind.

As darkness fell, my plan was made. I knew exactly what I had to do. I retraced my steps back to 24a West Park Avenue and let myself in once more to Mrs. G's apartment. I knew she would be returning soon from her weekend away, so I had to be quick. I felt guilty about being back there but had convinced myself I wasn't doing anything wrong.

Now, where would she keep the keys to D'Arcy's? I thought.

A stickler for tidiness, I attempted to put myself into Gigi Gerson's mind.

Where would she put them? Where would she hide them?

I hated myself for prowling through her belongings, then I remembered how cold it was on the city streets and told myself I would be done for if I attempted to stay out all night. The thought made me feel only slightly better. In her bedroom, I surveyed the scene. Her dresser drawers and bedside cabinet drawers were instantly eliminated from my search – way too obvious! I sat down on the edge of her enormous super King bed and calmed my mind for a moment. My heart had been racing and the clock was ticking. She would be back soon. I took a few deep breaths and calmed myself then said quietly and directly to myself and the universe, "Where are the keys to D'Arcy's Department Store."

Just then the phone rang. I jumped out of my skin. The phone went straight to the answering machine. It was a man's voice. He sounded very direct and spoke in a perfectly clipped tone that indicated he was very well educated. I surmised it was her lawyer. I looked at the time on the bedside clock, she would be back home in about half an hour.

Once again, I calmed my breathing and placed my sweat-stained palms on my knees. Then I scanned the room once more. My attention was caught by a silver canister containing Tiffany blue pens on the dressing table. I knew that Mrs. G wrote all her personal correspondence with these pens and there were always two or three laying on her desk at work at any given time. I walked over and pulled a bunch of the elegantly designed pens out of the silver holder and held them in my hands. They were weighty, defying their slimline look. As I reached out to place them back in the holder, I noticed a small bunch of silver keys at the bottom of the container. I took them out and opened a furled brown piece of paper that was attached to the key fob. The initials D.D.S. had been almost rubbed out.

Bingo!

I bolted out of the apartment, making sure to lock it before I left. Now, all I had to do was find one of those key cutting machines.

I didn't have to look long. New York was like that. You could get your hands on just about anything at any time of the day or night. It truly was the city that never slept. As I made my way back to Mrs. G's apartment, a creeping sense of anxiety washed over me...was I really going ahead with my plan? A gust of wind took my breath away as I pulled my scarf up over my mouth. There was my answer.

With the original set of keys delivered safely back to the apartment, I made my way to Queens on the subway. Holding my bag tightly in front of my chest, I noticed, not for the first time, the subway riders who spent a large portion of their day living a subterranean lifestyle. Now, I could see why. Who could blame them? Who in their right mind would want to face those freezing temperatures above ground? A solitary tear trickled down my cheek as I realized I was now in the same category. But what about Jackson? Was he too riding the subway to stay warm?

Just then an elderly woman of eastern European descent appeared in the carriage of commuters. I eyed her nervously as she proffered small bags of lavender for a dollar apiece. I reached in my jacket pocket and pulled out a five-dollar note. I didn't want her wares, but I wanted to give her the note. As the woman approached, she stood directly in front of me and smiled.

"A bag of lavender for you sweetie?"

Her kind smile warmed me as I offered her the note.

As she gathered up five bags of lavender, I interrupted.

"I don't want them...I just want you to have the money."

"That's very kind of you sweetie," she reassured, "But I want you to take one bag and keep it with you at all times."

Ok, then, I thought.

As we exchanged our gifts, her expression changed, "Courage is born in the face of adversity," she said quietly before moving on. I was gobsmacked.

I blushed then smiled back at her. "I know," I replied, and then she was gone.

I had reached my station, in more ways than one.

***

As I climbed the stairs lit by the last shards of daylight, I knew it would only be a short walk along Main Street to D'Arcy's Department Store. The throngs of customers would have departed by now and there would only be a few remaining customers left to annoy the hell out of the part-time staff, who were usually employed for their looks and not for the elevated standards of customer service, although I had to admit that Rose was a noted exception in that category.

I stood opposite the four-storey building and really saw it, perhaps for the first time. I took in its elegant late 19th century architectural adornments and noticed that the building was looking somewhat the worse for wear. The upkeep alone must have given Mrs. G many sleepless nights. As the clock struck 10:00pm, I stood in the shadows and watched on as Cecil, our beloved doorman locked the front door with his large cluster of keys. I hoped and prayed that the key I held in my hand was not a front door key. The CCTV man would have a field day!

Ever thankful for my skipped hat and woolen scarf, I bundled myself behind a pillar of the building I was taking shelter in and waited for the last remaining members of staff to leave. I stood there as long as I could. Once it appeared that no-one else would come out of the building, I made my move.

Deftly, I sprung across the road and walked on purpose by the front entrance. I walked a few steps north of the building then stopped to peer into a clothes shop window. There was no-one else around as I turned around and made my way back towards the department store that was going to be my home for the night. As I reached the side entrance, I put the key in the staff entrance door and held my breath. At first, the key would not turn. I looked around and still the coast was clear. I tried again. The key didn't budge. Then I remembered to pull the door towards me and twist the key at the same time. Success! The door opened. I stepped into the darkness, too afraid to switch on a light. Instead, I took out my mobile phone and illuminated my way up the fire exit stairs with bated breath. Thankfully, there was no sign of any stragglers in the building. I had the added advantage of knowing exactly where I was going…all the way to the fourth floor – home of electricals, wallpaper, interiors, and bedding. The fourth floor was also home to the Ladies loos, which would be very convenient during my overnight stay.

On arrival, feeling breathless through a combination of adrenalin and exertion, I stood in the shadows until I was absolutely sure there was no-one in the building, then I walked into the ladies' loos and changed into the pj's that Mrs. G had gifted me for Christmas. My hands were almost blue with cold as I warmed them under the dryer. My cheeks were ruddy with the cold and I looked a right old mess, but at least I had a roof over my head and had escaped the outdoor frozen temperatures. Gradually, I began to relax as my plan fell effortlessly into place. That's when I noticed it had begun to snow.

Those poor souls out there…

Exhausted from my day of traipsing the streets, I snuggled under the display bed duvet and drifted off to sleep.

***

"Be Jesus, Mary and Joseph, Willow! What are you doing here? You gave me the fright of my bloody life, you did!"

Jake O'Riordan stared at me as if he had seen a ghost. It took a moment or two to gather my thoughts and remember where I was.

"Shooosh! Please don't tell anyone Jake," I pleaded, "I had nowhere else to go."

"We can't be having this, Willow," Jake shook his head in disgust then stormed off.

I had never seen our normally mild-mannered cleaner look so pissed off.

Shit. He's going to blow my cover, I thought, as I frantically kicked off the covers and ran to the "Ladies" to get dressed. By the time he got back from wherever he went, I was looking fairly composed in a "rumpled clothes from yesterday" kind of way.

Jake returned, carrying a "Henry" the hoover in one hand and a paper carrier bag in the other. He sat down on the edge of the display bed and looked at me with an expression I had never seen before. To be perfectly honest, I had never paid Jake much attention at all, but now looking at him sitting across from me, it was obvious he held all the cards in this situation. It was up to him whether he kept my secret or blew my cover and I had no idea which way it was going to go.

He handed me the paper carrier bar.

"What's this?" I asked, looking inside.

"Coffee. Milk and two sugar. Correct?" he asked.

"But how did you know?" I asked, confused. *How the hell does he know I take two sugar in my coffee?*

Jake looked rile, "Never mind that. You've got some explaining to do."

I took a sip of the burning coffee and felt its warmth travel all the way to my toes.

"So, what happened, that you had to spend the night in your place of work? Were you drunk?" His question infuriated me.

"No! I bloody well was not," I replied indignantly.

"Don't be so uppity now…it's not unusual for you and Jackson to go out on the lash…now is it?"

Who the hell does he think he is? My father? I wondered.

It was the first time I really paid attention to Jake, of course, I had seen him working around the store, doing odd jobs for Mrs. G but I never bothered to find out anything about him or his job for that matter. He was always just there, in the background. I reckoned he was perhaps a year or two older than myself and he was maybe a couple of inches taller than me. When he handed me the paper bag, I noticed his hands were gnarled from hard labour; his were working hands, hands that were never shy of a day's hard work. I gathered he was angry with me for having put myself in a situation.

"What if there had been a fire? Eh? No-one would have known you were even in the building…no-one would have come to look for you!" he declared. He was right.

"Ok!" I snapped. "I get it! But it was better than sleeping on the streets."

Jake stared at me.

Shit!

"What do you mean – 'better than sleeping on the streets'?"

"Never mind," I said, full of indignation.

"Right," said Jake, and then he was off. "I've got work to do."

I felt bad. Real bad. I went into the "Ladies" and applied my makeup. There was no time for a shower now, not after my little tete-a-tete with Jake.

The shift passed uneasily with Jake and I ignoring each other. My problems were not over. Now that Jake knew my secret, I couldn't dare risk staying another night in the department store…and I had nowhere else to go. The store clock ticked relentlessly onwards towards 5:00pm, the hour my shift was due to finish. As I watched the hands of the clock march on, it was the first time in my life when I had wished for time to slow down.

To make matters worse, Isabella appeared in front of me.

"Can you smell something?" she held her nose as she said it. I had been careful to spray myself with J'adore Dior throughout the day, but I guessed my pit stains were now showing through my uniform dress. Thankfully, it was time for my shift to be over. I left D'Arcy's and made my way straight for the bus that would take me to the Empire State Building. The journey took just under an hour, allowing me to stay warm. For some strange reason, the building beckoned me. It was the only place in the city that I felt I could truly breathe. I took the lift all the way to the 102nd floor and looked out over the city through the safety glass covered windows. I realized then that I wanted to be out in the cold air, so I made my way down to the viewing platform on the 86th floor. It was so cold out there and even though I felt like I might flash freeze on the spot, the cold searing through my body made me feel instantly alive. I stayed out as long as I could endure it. There were a few young lovebirds holding hands and gazing out over the cityscape, and then I noticed a young man in his early 20's who appeared to have been stood up by his date. He eventually gave up and left, leaving me alone with only my thoughts for company. Looking out over the Hudson River and the Brooklyn Bridge, I remembered the reasons why I had always wanted to come here. The magical allure of New York had caught me in a stranglehold.

Immersed in my thoughts, I was soon distracted by a silhouette appearing out of the shadows. The man was holding a bucket and mop. He stopped mopping the floor and stood directly in front of me.

"Willow! What are you doing up here?"

It was Jake, the cleaner from D'Arcy's who appeared to be working job number two.

He ushered me in off the platform and into the warmth of the building.

"You're freezing. Stay here, I'll be back in a mo."

I stood there helpless, numbed and chilled to the core. I was so cold, I couldn't think.

Jake returned with a plastic cup of vending machine hot chocolate, "Here, drink this." I took the cup willingly, but my hands were frozen inside my gloves and I almost dropped the contents all over the floor.

"Steady up! You trying to give me more work?" Jake broached a smile, timidly at first, as he helped me hold the cup. "Now drink up and then we'll talk…I've just got to take this bucket and mop back to the storeroom first."

I did as I was told. I didn't have an ounce of energy left to put up a fight.

When Jake returned five minutes later, he found me sobbing into my gloves. I was scared and lonely and had no clue what to do next.

Jake sat on the chair beside me and put one arm around me, "Look, everything's gonna be ok, pet. You've had a rough time of it, and we're all surprised you are still here, we thought you would have given up and gone home yonks ago."

"You did?" This revelation shocked me.

"Yes! Believe me, most people would have got on the first flight home when they found out about the baby…but you stayed," Jake paused, "And I admire that."

I didn't know what to say. It was a shock to hear about other people's viewpoints of the whole situation and there was me battling my way through it all, without any idea of what anyone else thought of the situation.

"It's not in my nature to give up," I responded.

Jake chuckled, "Yes! That's been noted." Jake took the empty cup from my hand. "Right, stand up and come with me," he demanded.

"Why? Where are we going?" I asked.

"You'll see, but first there's someone waiting to meet you downstairs."

"Uh oh! Don't like the sound of that," I said, "Who is it?" I asked.

Jake gave me a wry smile, "You'll see in a minute."

The tension between us was palpable as we stepped into the lift and descended the 86 floors to the ground floor. As we rode the lift in silence, I felt a sensation of relief when the doors finally slid open.

Jake smiled nervously at me, "I'll leave you two to it…it's my guess you've got a lot to talk about."

I drew Jake a look and cussed under my breath; no wonder he hadn't wanted to tell me.

I stepped out and stared at Rick while Jake made his excuses to leave. I could have slapped him for putting me in this situation with Rick.

Rick appeared perplexed, "So, what's been going on? Jake tells me you've been sleeping rough in D'Arcy's."

"It was only one night," I responded coolly. "I had nowhere else to go."

Rick looked incredulous. "You know you could have stayed with me…" he paused, as he realized his words were not going down well.

I threw him the dirtiest look I could muster.

"Yeah! Mighty cozy that would have been," I scolded. "Me, you and your pregnant girlfriend."

Rick stared at his feet.

"I'm sorry, Willow. I never meant for it all to turn out like this." For a moment, he looked agitated, like he really meant what he was saying. "I feel responsible for the way things have turned out," he said as he fidgeted with his coat pocket. He handed me a thick brown envelope.

"What's this?" I asked, "More paperwork from Homeland Security?"

"No. It's five thousand dollars. Enough money to get you a deposit and two months' rent on a room somewhere."

I shooed his hand away from me.

"I'm not taking your money," I said, feeling disgusted with him.

He looked at me, mystified, "It's our money, Willow," he said. "I have some very generous relatives. They were happy to see me finally married and settled…until I went and fucked everything up."

For a fleeting moment, I felt sorry for him.

"Go on. Take it. Please," he demanded as he pushed the envelope into my hand.

I noticed Jake appear within view, he nodded over, encouraging me to open the envelope. As he walked towards us, I felt like I had an ally in the situation.

"I've found you a nice hotel room for the rest of the week, and I've a few contacts in the community. Someone might know someone with a room available to rent…leave it with me." Jake said.

"Ok." I relented. "Thank you. Both of you." I felt a wave of relief wash over me. Rick approached and handed me the envelope then hugged me tightly. The familiar waft of cedar and vetiver clung to me as I reciprocated.

I turned and looked over to see Jake waiting on me.

"Right madam. Let's get you to your hotel room. You'll be wanting to get settled before it gets any later.

"You got me a hotel room?" I asked.

"Well, you're not bloody well spending another night in D'Arcy's, are you?" He asked sternly.

I clutched the brown envelope tightly and smiled to myself, "No, I'm guessing I'm not." I replied.

The hotel was a charming boutique-style hotel in the Flushing neighbourhood of Queens. It was located a walkable distance from the department store and was surrounded by a myriad of restaurants, cafes, and bars. Jake handed me over to the receptionist, introducing me as his cousin from Scotland. Then he turned and winked at me before whispering, "They think you're related to me; they'll take good care of you."

I was secretly impressed by this "powerhouse" of a man with two jobs who was apparently well regarded in his local hood. It was obvious by his mannerisms that he "took no shit" and demanded respect everywhere he went, so why was he working in a lowly job at Darcy's Department Store? I thought. As if reading my mind, Jake saw me into my room and then made to leave, "I've got to see a man about a dog," he laughed. "But I'll be back in 20 to take you to the local bar and introduce you to the barman," he stated, "Oh...and not meaning to be cheeky or anything but you might want to spruce yourself up a bit after spending the night in D'Arcy's. I blushed as he indicated towards the shower, that was visible through the open bathroom door.

As soon as he left, I stripped off and jumped into the shower, scrubbing myself with the hotel edition verbena soap. It was a delicious experience to feel clean again after a night of sleeping rough. Then I wrapped myself in the sumptuous white bath sheets before throwing myself on top of the bed. I realized then that Jake had caught my attention in a rather unexpected way.

Who was this Irish man with the two jobs, who seemed to know all about me, and yet I knew nothing about him?

That night I made it my mission to find out as much as I could about him. Except there was one problem. I had no fresh clothes to put on. All my personal belongings had been left in Jackson's apartment.

Shit! Shit! Shit! Aaaargh!

There was a knock at the door. It must be him. I wrapped myself up in the bath sheet and made the precaution of looking through the tiny circular security window. Yes. It was Jake. He had returned. Mortified, I let him in.

Jake looked me up and down and blushed slightly.

"Er…would you like me to wait outside while you get dressed?"

"Well, that's just the problem. I don't have any clothes to change into," I explained as I clutched onto the towel with grit determination.

Jake chuckled then gathered his thoughts.

"My sister is much the same size as yourself. Give me ten minutes and I'll go grab something from her…she'll not mind…honest."

"But…!" I hesitated, but it was too late…he was gone.

"Oh my God! This is a disaster," I sat back down on top of the bed and turned on the TV.

As promised, ten minutes later, Jake returned to my hotel room clutching a brown paper carrier bag. He looked very pleased with himself as he poured the contents on top of the bed.

"I got you these. Brenda says she doesn't want them back. You've to keep them," he said smiling, guessing by all accounts that he had done a great job. Little did he know this situation was equivalent to every woman's nightmare. I prayed to God above that there would be at least a few items of black clothing but there was nothing of the sort. Instead, my bed resembled a kaleidoscope of colour…everything from shocking pink to lime green. I attempted to put on a brave face as I pulled the heaped jumble apart.

"Do you mind giving me a few minutes?" I asked Jake, as he looked on.

He made his way to the door, "Not at all. I'll meet you at the bar in 10 minutes, is that OK?"

I nodded.

Twenty-five minutes later, I made my way through the busy lobby towards the crowded bar area. The guests parted at the seams as I made my appearance. My wet hair had been pulled back in a ponytail, while the bubblegum pink mohair jumper skimmed my belly button. An expanse of bare untoned midriff was exposed to the crowd, but worse still, the lime green leggings did little for the imagination as they clung tightly to my nether regions, exposing VPL and a camel toe. I had no choice but to put my work shoes on once more. I had not an ounce of "warpaint" in my arsenal and was forced to go barefaced, something I had never done since the age of 14 years old. I was quite simply mortified.

As Jake turned around to hand me a glass of wine, he erupted into peals of laughter.

"Be Jesus Willow! It's 1994 all over again."

"Shut up!" I yelled, as Madonna sang "Like a Virgin." I grabbed the glass of wine from him and gulped it down, if I was going to have to parade around looking like this then I may as well be drunk and not care. Jake watched on in awe as I ordered a bottle of wine.

"You're some girl, Willow…you're some girl and I'm guessing there is something rather cool about you."

He took off his overcoat and placed it carefully over my shoulders then led me down Main Street to introduce me to the rest of the O'Riordan clan.

The next morning, I awoke with a pounding headache and a mouth the texture of sandpaper. I opened my eyes and squinted at my surroundings. The hotel room had all the trappings of a night on the lash – empty beer cans and a half-full bottle of white wine lay strewn across the coffee table.

One by one, the memories flooded in. I recalled being introduced to Jake's older sisters: Brenda and Colette. Both were married and in their early 40s and both had jumped at the chance of a mid-week drinking session into the wee hours. The local pub had given us a "lock-in" whereby we stayed on drinking longer than the official bylaws allowed.

I pulled back the duvet and was shocked to see I was still wearing the atrocious outfit from the night before, except the shocking pink top had a red wine stain over the left boob area.

"Yikes!"

I padded into the bathroom and checked my D'Arcy's uniform dress for smells of dampness left over from the previous night's handwashing. There were none. The outfit was bone dry. For that, at least, I was thankful.

I wondered how Jake was feeling. He was rather the worse for wear when he dropped me off at the hotel at 3:00am. A smile erupted across my face as I remembered how he had got up to sing a karaoke song for me. *What was it? The Irish Rover? Yes. That was it.*

He sang the whole song at me. I attempted to remember the lyrics, but the memory of his cheeky grin foreshadowed everything else.

Willow Campbell...are you falling for a penniless Irishman? No! No! No! Absolutely not...never happening.

I spent the next half an hour attempting to get ready for work while wrestling with my conscience. The longer the fight went on, the clearer it became to me I was losing.

An hour later, I took up my position behind the counter at Blake's Apothecary. It was lonely without Jackson making me laugh, but somehow in the space of 24 hours, Jake O' Riordan had come to represent another distraction.

As the day progressed, I became more and more aware that perhaps Jake was avoiding me. I had barely seen him all day long, and when I did, he did little more than smile over at me in a kind of shy way. At 4:55pm, he finally made an appearance in front of my counter.

"I'll meet you outside in ten minutes," he said directly.

"Oh…ok then, where are we going?" I asked.

"Manhattan."

"What? Why are we going there?" I asked, but Jake had already turned to leave the Beauty Hall floor. I packed up my belongings and completed my handover with Rose who would be staying on until 10:00pm.

"See you tomorrow, Rose."

I rushed over to the staff changing room and collected my belongings from my locker. I had acquired three bags of shopping during my lunch hour and had amassed three new outfits to wear. I had used my staff discount, so I didn't feel quite so guilty about spending $300 from the money that Rick had given me.

I stepped out into the twilight. A thin layer of ice had set on the pavement, casting a magical winter glow on the street. Jake was waiting on me.

"Explain again, why we are going to Manhattan?" I asked, nervously.

"Well your money's not going to last very long if you pay for a hotel every night, so we need to get you set up in an apartment."

My pulse quickened.

"But Manhattan? I'll never be able to afford that!"

Jake grinned at me, "Now that's the spirit, Willow. What's that song you are always singing? "I've got a pocket full of dreams?"

I smiled back unaware that he had noticed my dreadful singing.

"Hasn't it always been your ambition to live there? I remember you relaying the story of how you arrived at Rick's apartment and you thought you were going to be staying in Uptown Manhattan…"

I blushed at my own naiveté.

"That all seems like such a long time ago."

Jake stopped in his tracks and stared hard at me, "I think he sold you up the river, Willow." I looked away.

"He's not completely at fault," I said, "I should have been wiser. Maybe got to know him a bit better before I married him…I guess he swept me off my feet." The conversation made me feel uncomfortable. No-one likes owning up to their own misgivings.

"Are you over him now Willow?" Jake asked, staring hard at me.

Why is he asking me this? I wondered. I shuffled from one foot to the other, not knowing what to say.

Jake looked wounded. "Sorry. None of my business. I've no right to pry into your private life."

Jake changed his tone to his default "cheeky Irishman" but there was something about the way in which he spoke that unnerved me, and if I were completely honest, he did seem to know rather a lot about me.

We had arrived at the subway station that would take us from Queens to Manhattan. As we took our seats in preparation for the journey, Jake looked me up and down.

"I must admit Willow, you're looking a lot better than you did last night!" he laughed.

"Cheeky git!" I swiped his arm playfully.

"The black is way more becoming than the lime green and shocking pink."

"I was channeling Madonna, don't knock it!"

"That reminds me," he said, "I forgot to tell you that we're going to her old neighbourhood."

"We are?" I shouted, "I've been a fan of her…for like ever!"

"Well, you're going to love this."

He handed me a sheet of paper with an apartment address in Hell's Kitchen.

"What's this?"

"I found out there's an apartment available in her old building."

"No! Never!" I hugged Jake tightly, squeezing the air out of him.

"Now, don't get too excited. You haven't got it yet and you have to meet the landlord."

"I do?"

"She'll want to interview you, make sure you are legit…and whatever you do, don't mention the night you spent sleeping in D'Arcy's," he winked at me with a knowing smile.

"As if I would! What do you take me for!"

"Just be on your best behavior. That's all I'm asking," he said.

I couldn't get over the extent to which Jake was going to help me.

"What time is the meeting?" I asked.

Jake looked at his watch, "20 minutes from now."

"What? But you haven't given me any time to prepare!" I called, brushing my hair like a maniac and checking my reflection in the tiny handheld mirror. I took out my red lipstick and attempted to apply it as we trundled along underground.

"Calm down, you look smashing the way you are…and I didn't give you much notice because I didn't want you to get wound up and nervous."

I laughed, "Well, that's exactly what I am now!"

Jake attempted to comfort, "Look, you'll be fine…just be…you." He smiled at me warmly, causing me to feel a little self-conscious.

Why have I never noticed this man? I thought. We trundled on in a comfortable silence, that rare kind of silence that requires no words, no talking for talking's sake. At one point, Jake looked like he was nodding off, I smiled to myself as I analysed his features in that makeup artist kind of way. He had a dimple on his right cheek and his Celtic skin was awash with freckles. His rugged complexion hinted at many years of working outdoors in the sunshine. But his hands were the biggest giveaway to the kind of life he had lived. This man was clearly a worker. Hard work was no stranger to him. I wanted to nourish his parched skin with my shea butter hand cream.

But I guessed he would say no to the thought of using hand cream. I placed my head on his shoulder and relaxed, lulled by the motion of the train. I hoped he wouldn't think I was being forward…

"Willow! Wake up…we're here!"

I immediately opened my eyes and stared at my surroundings. Jake was dragging me up out of my seat and bundling me towards the carriage door. He gripped my hand tightly and I liked it.

"We've got five minutes to get there," he called back to me as we snaked through the rush hour crowd going in the opposite direction. As we reached Hell's Kitchen hood, we stopped for a breath of air.

"You might want to…er…fix your eyeliner before we go in," he suggested.

"Why? what's the matter?" I asked, searching for the handheld mirror that was lying at the bottom of my bag.

"It's nothing really…just a little smudged, that's all," I noticed a thick black spot on the collar of Jake's white polo shirt and realized I must have smudged my makeup when I fell asleep briefly on the subway.

Jake's eyes darted towards his right shoulder, "Aw no…have you managed to get it on me too?"

"Sorry. Didn't mean to," I apologized.

Jake made a vain attempt at rubbing the mark then looked at me, "Don't worry about it. I kind of like it," he said as the familiar dimple appeared on his right cheek.

I pushed his shoulder lightly, "You're mad, you are. Come on…let's get going."

***

The meeting with Mrs. Canhill lasted all of five minutes. She showed me around the tiny apartment on the 8th floor of the building, asked me if I wanted it and then gave me a receipt and a tenancy form to sign. She handed me a set of keys and told me the apartment would be available the following day, once the cleaners had been in. I had heard of horror stories surrounding the act of signing tenancy leases in New York City and couldn't believe how stress-free my experience had been. I wondered how well Jake and Mrs. Canhill knew each other, but at the end of the day, I finally had a place to stay, a place all my own in one of the buzziest parts of New York. It if was good enough for Madonna in the 80s then it was good enough for me.

As we departed the building, Jake stopped in his tracks and stared at me, "Seriously, Willow, do you like it?" he asked.

"Jake, you've no idea how much I LOVE it. I'm gonna make it my own and call it my 'home'"

"That's the spirit. It's a bit rough around the edges but once you've put your mark on it, it'll be gas. Now come on, let's get you back to Queens, I'll put you on the subway and then I'll head over to my cleaning job."

"Are you working in the Empire State Building tonight?"

"Yeah, just a short shift…only four hours, I'm helping one of my colleagues out."

"That's nice of you."

"His kid's got cancer. I do what I can to help him keep his job."

I was stopped dead in my tracks at this explanation.

"Medical bills are through the roof. You can't even begin to imagine, Willow."

"Dear God. That's awful…" I was catapulted out of my own world of worries by this news. "Anything I can do to help?" I asked. It was the least I could do to offer my services.

"How's your mopping skills?" he asked, dimple flashing cheekily.

"Top notch! The best on the block," I laughed.

"Come with me then. If anything, it'll make the shift go faster."

Two hours later, as I stood once again on the Observatory

Platform, 86 floors high in the winter sky, I thought how magical and mysterious life can be. I thought back to the yellow book and the urge to take a chance in life. I hadn't yet got off the rollercoaster of life, but I was enjoying the endless twists and turns that life threw at me.

"Penny for them?" Jake interrupted my thoughts, "You missed a bit," he said as he pointed to a dry patch on the platform floor.

"Cheeky!"

24

WINTER FLURRY

On January 12th, I had rushed towards the safety of the subway station just as the heavens opened. A winter storm had been forecast for the remainder of the evening and into the early hours of the following morning. As Jake and I huddled together, shaking the remnants of the ice storm from our winter coats, I wondered if it wise for Jake to volunteer for his colleague tonight.

"Are you sure you're going to be OK?" I asked. I looked at the data on my phone. "It's already registering -6 Degrees Centigrade, what's it going to be like up there? It'll be like -20, you'll freeze to death."

"Ever the optimist, eh?" Jake turned away. He looked faintly angry at my suggestion for him not to go. "He'll already be at the hospital right now…they're doing a lumbar puncture on the poor kid."

"Sorry. I didn't realise." I felt bad.

"I already told you what was happening, you couldn't have been listening to me," Jake chastised.

What's bugging him? I wondered.

We continued for the next few stops in silence. I said "goodbye" to Jake. I wasn't in the mood to accommodate other people's bad moods. It was a relief to reach Hell's Kitchen and make my way alone through the throngs of commuters and tourists. As I reached my building, I noticed there was a "Madonna" tour lining up outside. It was the one facet of life that I didn't enjoy about living in this part of the city, but hey! Ho! I chose to live here so I'd just have to get used to it. A bunch of pretty Japanese girls in their late teens had dressed to look the part of Madonna during her "Holiday" time. They wore flirty short skirts and had numerous rows of beads wrapped around their wrists. I laughed as I heard them sing the star's songs in their Japanese accent.

I huddled under my thick coat and thought of how cold they must be right now, but they didn't appear to be too bothered. I let myself into the building and traversed the eight floors to my apartment.

As I opened the door, I was immediately hit with an icy blast of cold; it felt colder in my apartment than it did outside. I had left the living room window open and now the curtains were flapping around wildly at the window.

"Shit! Stupid idiot!" I said to myself, as I ran to slam the window shut. I turned the gas fire on full and boiled the kettle, all the while keeping my winter coat on. The earlier conversation with Jake had bothered me. I hadn't wanted to come across so crass. I should have known that the young boy had been getting his treatment today, but I had got caught up in my own stuff and hadn't paid attention.

I hope he doesn't think I'm shallow, I thought.

I switched off the kettle and turned off the gas heater then left the apartment wearing the same coat I had arrived in. Back on street level, I trudged through the snow to the subway and made my way towards 49th Street. It was just a short hop on the subway to Herald Square and then a short stroll to the Empire State Building, but the journey time took almost half an hour door to door as I trudged through snow that was beginning to lie deep.

"Damn this weather!" I thought. As I entered the building, I braced myself for the temperatures I would face 86 flights up.

I must be off my freakin head, I thought. I searched for Jake on the 86th floor but there was no sign of him. Perhaps he saw sense after all. I thought. There was no-one around. The tourists had left for the day and no-one else in their right mind wanted to be so high up in the atmosphere during a winter storm. I turned around and made my way to leave, just as I heard a voice call my name. It was Jake. He looked upset.

"What's the matter?" I asked.

Jake shook his head and stared at his snow-covered boots. "It's not good, Willow."

I felt my knees buckle slightly. I knew instantly he was referring to the child, Billy. "What can we do?" I asked. "There must be something we can do to help."

"They need to find $35000 for a new treatment plan. It's the boy's last hope."

I shuddered, "Where are they gonna find that kind of money?"

Jake shook his head in despair. "I've no clue. What about you, do you know any rich benefactors?"

I shook my head. No-one in my world had that kind of money to give away.

"Do you want a hot chocolate? I've only got another hour to go and then I'll be finished." He asked, swiftly changing the subject

"Yes, but let me help you and then we can both get out of here," I offered.

Jake touched my arm, "Look, about before…I'm sorry for snapping at you…I didn't mean to…just got a lot on my mind, you know?" That was the first time it struck me that Jake would be losing his job too.

"It's ok. I can see you have a lot on your mind," I comforted.

The remainder of the cleaning shift passed quickly as we shared the tasks of the job. There were no tourists to get in the way of the mopping and I donned a pair of plastic gloves in preparation for emptying the bins on the observation platform. Once the job was done, I threw the gloves in the trash bin and cleaned my hands with the hand sanitizer. The snow was falling horizontally at this height as the wind blew ferociously from the east. I looked over towards the Hudson River and drank in the intoxicating views. There was something truly magical about being up the Empire State Building during a snowstorm.

"Thanks for helping tonight, you did a grand job, so you did," said Jake.

"It was nothing really," I said, feeling a tad despondent at the news. "35 thousand dollars? How can that be? Who has that type of money lying around?".

We had reached Herald Street underground and were about to go our separate ways when Jake noticed a sign saying that his subway line to Queens 104 Street would be out of order for the duration of the evening.

"Shit! What am I gonna do now?" he asked staring at me.

"You'll have to stay with me," I said.

"No. I can't do that," he responded. "That wouldn't be right."

What is the matter with this guy? I thought. It's a freakin snowstorm and it's now 15 degrees below freezing.

"Fine. Well, sleep out in the snow then," I said huffily. "See how long you last out there."

Jake relented. "Are you sure that's Ok with you?" he asked. "I don't want to put you out or anything."

"Look. After everything you've done for me, it's the least I can do for you," I smiled, bad mood lifting slightly. "I'll make you up a nice bed on the couch," I said. Jake smiled.

"Ok then. Hell's Kitchen it is," he said as we jumped on the subway to my neck of the woods.

By the time we arrived back at the apartment, it had gone past 10:00pm.

"Let me order us some takeaway and a nice bottle of wine," Jake offered.

"If you like…I'll put the kettle on."

As I stood alone in the cold kitchen, I pondered my situation. I was fond of Jake, but circumstances had hardened me towards getting into another relationship, and besides, I was still technically married to Rick.

I fetched the spare duvet wrapped in a floral cabbage print by Cath Kidston and placed it on top of the couch. The apartment had not yet warmed up and I could tell that Jake was still cold.

"Can I get you another blanket or something?"

I noticed that he was chittering as he sat on the edge of the couch.

"I don't know what's the matter with me, Willow, but I can't seem to heat up. My hands and feet are like blocks of ice," he looked worried.

"Yes. I can see that," I said slowly as I quickly googled the signs of hypothermia. Jake was very pale. I felt like I should act quickly.

"Lie down on the couch," I instructed. "I need to get you out of these clothes," Jake was growing paler and shook incessantly as I pulled off the outer layers of his clothing. He still found the energy to joke with me, "Now don't you be taking advantage of me, Willow." As worried as I was, I started to laugh a little.

"Fat chance," I replied.

I rushed off and fetched my faux fur hot water bottle and a pair of the thickest socks I could find. I lay the hot water bottle on his stomach between his t-shirt and under his jumper. Then I bundled every blanket and duvet I had on top of him. I turned the thermostat up to the highest temperature then made Jake drink from a huge mug of hot tea.

Ever so gradually the heat began to return to his body as his pallor improved.

"I think I'm getting you back, Jake," I stated, as I checked his symptoms with my first aid page on the iPad. "I think you're going to be ok."

Jake lay on the couch and stared at me. His stare lasted a second or two longer than it should have. I looked away. I turned off the light and bid him goodnight.

"If you feel bad during the night, you know where I am," I said, as I rushed off to my room.

I shut the bedroom door behind me and stood for a moment, staring at my surroundings.

"Nope. This is not happening," I said sternly to myself. "I am not falling for this man."

I jumped into bed and pulled the last remaining thin blanket over me. I wondered what the yellow book would have to say about this situation.

Early the next morning, I was awoken by the sound of pots and pans being clattered in the kitchen. The events of the previous night slowly came back to me as I remembered I had a house guest. I pulled the thin blanket up under my chin just as there was a knock on the door.

"Willow? Are you awake? I made you some coffee."

"Come in," I said coyly, feeling embarrassed that Jake was once again seeing me in my pj's.

He placed the mug of coffee down on the bedside table then scanned the small room.

"Jeez. I feel bad. You must have been freezing last night. I'm sorry for taking all your bedding."

I smiled, "You needed it more than me."

"I guess I did, didn't I? Feeling grand today though…and er…thanks for looking after me so well last night."

"It's nothing. I 'd do anyone a favour," I smiled.

"Oh, by the way, we have the day off. D'Arcy's is closed for the day. The snowstorm was so bad last night that there's no way we're gonna get through to Queens this morning."

I brightened. "Really?"

"So, I figured...how about a nice walk along by the Hudson? Then I'll take you for breakfast at one of my favourite Italian cafes."

"That sounds nice...but are you sure you want to brace the cold after last night?" I asked, concerned about his health.

Jake flexed his muscles. "You're looking at tough Irish stock, Willow, a little snowstorm is not going to stop me," he said.

"Ok. Then out you go and let me get dressed," I commanded. I closed the door behind him and caught my reflection in the bedroom mirror. There was a smile on my face.

***

The winter walk alongside the choppy shores of the Hudson lasted a little under ten minutes. As we neared Gino's Italian Eatery, I exhaled a sigh of relief. I could bear the cold no more.

On arrival, Jake bundled me into a window-side table. It had the best view in the house. Jake handed me a grubby, fingerprint stained, plastic-covered menu and suggested the Eggs Benedict. I chose the Bruschetta and a black coffee. As the waitress took our order, a youngish male in his early 30s approached us.

"What's up Jake? Haven't seen you in a long time." The two men high fived and hugged like a pair of long-lost brothers. Then Gino turned his attention to me, "Who is this then, your girlfriend?" I blushed as Jake blundered, "This is my good friend, Willow. She's from Glasgow."

Gino looked at me and then at Jake and cracked a wicked grin but chose to say nothing.

"Glasgow, eh? You'll know my uncle Roberto then?"

"I hardly think so," I said. "It's a big city."

"He runs an Italian food store just off Buchanan Street...you'll know when you see it." He trailed off, "Look, I'll leave you two love birds alone...anything you need, you call me Jake."

I didn't know who was more embarrassed, Jake or me.

So, this is how we look? I thought. Like lovebirds? Shit!

Jake took a pew in the seat opposite me and offered a quiet apology. "Sorry about that," he said, "he gets a bit carried away with himself sometimes."

Jake appeared like he regretted his decision to bring me into the café and I didn't for the life of me know how to turn the situation around. We ate our brunch in silence, staying perhaps a little more over 20 minutes.

As we stepped out into the street, Jake pulled up his collar and hugged me lightly, "I'd best be off, Willow. I'll see you tomorrow at work."

My heart surged with disappointment. "Ok then," I hesitated, looking at him, "See you tomorrow then." We both went our separate ways.

Willow Campbell, what the fuck is going on with you?

25

BEING FABULOUS

It was a bitterly cold morning in early February. Mrs. G had been indicted for harbouring illegals in her store and had been sentenced to six months behind bars at the York Correctional Institution in Connecticut. We had all been taking it in turns to call her as she continued to organise the New York Makeup Artistry Competition from the stark surroundings of her cell. Overall, her spirits were high considering she was about to lose everything she had taken decades to build up.

"Did you follow up with Carlotta? What time is she due to arrive at the airport?" she asked during one of her terse phone calls.

"Yes, she's arriving at 4:30 tomorrow afternoon."

"Will she have an entourage with her? Is she arriving alone or will some of her team be with her?"

"As far as I know, she'll be arriving alone. Rose has arranged for a car to go pick her up, but you know Carlotta…she'll be wanting to stop off uptown to meet up with some of her celeb friends."

Mrs. G replied, "Yes, I heard *The Muse* is in town this week."

My heart missed a beat.

"*The Muse*? Is that who I think it is? No! It can't be! "I yelled happily. Is she coming along too?" I bellowed, attracting the attention of the other workers in the staff room.

"Who knows? They're best friends, aren't they?" she replied nonchalantly as if talking about Carlotta and the supermodel known as *The Muse* was an everyday conversation for her.

I tried to envision doing a makeover on the world's top supermodel, watched over by the world's best Makeup Artist. Mrs. G interrupted my daydream.

"I think it's time for you to go now," she said.

I looked over my shoulder to see Isabella staring back at me. She was right, my call was up, and I didn't want to spend any longer on the phone and get Mrs. G reprimanded or myself, for that matter.

Mrs. G sighed, letting her stoic guard down for a few revealing seconds.

"Now you have all the instructions in your head, haven't you? Carlotta likes Valdo so make sure the office wine refrigerator is full and you can use the crystal glasses that I keep in a box in my office."

"I've got it all under control. Don't worry," I replied, figuring the more confidently I dealt with proceedings the more content Mrs. G would feel.

. "I'll call you next week when it's all over and done with," I responded

"After all this hard work, you better win that trophy – you hear me?"

"I'll do my best Mrs. Gerson."

***

It felt good to hear Mrs. G in high spirits considering the circumstances, and it felt even better to be regarded as her go-to-girl for all things concerning the makeup competition. I knew Mrs. G was rooting for me and I didn't want to let her or myself down.

I opened my makeup bag and repainted my lipstick

No matter which set of circumstances you find yourself in there's no excuse for not being fabulous.

At the end of my shift, I walked a few steps to the subway and caught the underground train to my new apartment in Hell's Kitchen. A multitude of thoughts rushed through my head as I deduced that New York certainly seemed to be rubbing off on me.

In the short time since I had moved into my new accommodation, I had painted the interior white and added a bold hue of colour with velvet accessories bought with my staff discount at D'Arcy's. I had chosen a regal royal blue to accent the tiny living room area and had descended into frou-frou girly pink in the bathroom. I imagined changing out the bland white subway tiles for art deco pink outlined by a gold-hued grout but I knew that was never going to happen so I added pops of colour any way I could. The result was a calming ambiance and a welcome escape from the busy city streets of West Manhattan.

Each morning, I awoke and had to pinch myself that one of my ambitions in life had come true – a Manhattan address. I kept the yellow book close by my bed. It was a stark reminder of how we really are the masters of our own destiny…with a few helpers along the way.

The only downside was the distance between Jake and I. After we had been referred to as "lovebirds" by his friend, we both backed off from each other. I hadn't wanted to become involved with another man and I'm guessing Jake had his own reasons for keeping his distance. It was a shame. We had both been getting along so well.

26

CAT FLICK

Carlotta strode up and down the aisles of D'Arcy's beauty hall, her flame of red hair falling in voluptuous waves as she navigated her way around the contestants. We were all held in an almost hypnotic trance, watching her as she graced the walkways. No one could believe that Mrs. G held such sway over one of the world's leading makeup artists and had gotten her to fly all the way over to New York from England to judge our competition. It seemed incredible to us but, knowing Mrs. G as I did now, I reckoned these two must have met up more than once in the past because nothing seemed to be too much trouble for Carlotta Rossellini.

It was obvious to me that Mrs. G had been giving orders from her cell room, as every detail of the competition had been thought out in advance and nothing had been left to chance. I sat in front of my makeup table patiently waiting for my model who was going to be sitting in the director's chair. It was a rule of the competition that no one would see their model until the day of the competition, which only served to heighten the anxiety levels even further.

The press had already arrived and had positioned themselves near the podium where the prizes would be presented. I spotted the photographer and reporter who had initially leaked the story to the press, but I pretended not to recognise them. It was one more situation than I could deal with right now and I had to focus on the task ahead of me.

Over to the side of me were three other makeup artists all of whom represented their New York stores: there was Glenda, a tall brunette beauty from Macy's who had a 15-year reputation in town, Jane from Nordstrom, and Lora, the youngest one from Saks Fifth Avenue. Word on the shop floor was that these three women represented the crème de la crème of New York makeup artistry talent.

Lost in thought, I flicked specks of pink peony powder from my workstation and sorted my brushes for the tenth time that hour.

"Excuse me, but are you Willow?"

I looked up to see Carlotta Rossellini staring back at me. Her eyes sparkled and her smile contained a hint of mirth as if she knew something I didn't.

"Yes, that's me," I replied. *Oh My God! It's her!*

What have I done to deserve this privilege?

"Very pleased to meet you," Carlotta held out her hand for me to shake it, "Gigi has told me a lot about you."

"All good, I hope?" I asked.

I braced myself for her answer, but Carlotta was the consummate professional, careful not to entangle herself in any situations that could be misconstrued as favouritism.

"That's for me to know and for you to find out," she replied cheekily. Carlotta laughed and then winked, "I'll be bringing your model out shortly, just as soon as everyone has settled down a little."

"Fantastic! I'm excited to finally meet her."

"You'll not be disappointed – that's for sure!"

"Willow…"

I turned around to see Carlotta holding hands with the world's most recognisable supermodel.

"Nadia got held up in traffic, so this young lady has agreed to stand in as your model today. I hope you don't mind?"

I looked at Carlotta who was smiling back at me, enjoying every second, as I experienced the biggest shock of my life.

You hope I don't mind? You hope that I don't mind?!?

I gulped, speechless. I couldn't get a freakin' sound out of my mouth. It took all my might just to smile. Inside I was trembling, I was going to be doing a makeover on one of the most photographed women in the world. Me? How could this be?

I thought about Mrs. G sitting in her cell.

Had she engineered this?

The Muse smiled and asked if she could sit down. Her feet were aching, and she was jetlagged. She told me she was looking forward to sitting down and doing nothing for 45 minutes, getting proper rest. She asked if she could have a glass of coke—she said she might even give me some suggestions on her eyeliner if that was OK.

Carlotta had already left at this point to attend to some other pre-competition problem that needed solving, leaving me to navigate my way around a situation I would never have dreamed of finding myself in – applying makeup to a supermodel.

I needn't have worried. I was as immediately at ease with her London accent as she was with my Glaswegian one. She told me about the Scottish friends she hung around with and how she regularly came up to stay in the Scottish Highlands, just to get away from it all. In turn, I regaled her with stories of how I came to befriend a Londoner in New York.

I did make a mental note not to discuss my situation with Rick, as I knew that she'd had problems with her men in the past and I was sure this was not the right time to broach *that* subject.

Carlotta took to the podium to make her opening speech about how honoured she was to be invited to open the first National Retail Makeup Artistry Competition. She alluded to how Gigi Gerson supported and nurtured the careers of makeup artists in New York, while still managing to expertly gloss over the fact that Mrs. G was doing jail time. I'm sure the press would figure that one out for themselves.

Then we were off. The clock was ticking and there was no time to spare. As I cleansed and toned my model's skin, I thought about the amount of time she must have spent in the makeup chair having her makeup applied by the world's best artists, and now it was my turn. I just hoped I was up to the task.

My hands were trembling slightly as I applied the cat flick synonymous with the supermodel.

I had never performed a makeover on such an exquisite face before. I was fascinated by the bone structure under her smooth porcelain skin and with each second, I became entranced at how her face seemed to transform before my eyes.

I lit the tops of her cheekbones, making sure that the highlighter didn't distract too much from her natural beauty, and applied a little concealer to the inner corners of her cat-like eyes. My model was completely at ease in the chair and I could tell that she really was exhausted from all the travelling she had done over the last few weeks. For her, jumping on a jet to get to work was the equivalent of me jumping on the nearest subway and travelling into the city.

Carlotta had made it very clear to the photographers that they weren't allowed to come near the models while they were in the chair. It suddenly struck me that for someone like her, who was relentlessly hounded by cameras, either by camera-toting members of the public or the paparazzi, my little makeover chair, for a short time, represented peace, quiet, and safety away from prying eyes. The only person who could come near us during the makeover was Carlotta, herself.

Twenty minutes into the makeover, *The Muse* began to emerge from her slumbering state. Over the years, she had mastered the skill of snoozing while sitting upright, but I sensed she was beginning to get antsy.

"Oops, do you mind if I go for a pee break?" she asked as I finished preparing a blend of eye shadow colours.

"Yes, of course. The toilets are just over there to the right," I stated, almost relieved that she would be leaving me for a few moments.

"Perfect! Thanks."

With my model away at the bathroom and Carlotta scrutinising the other contestants, I had five minutes to finally exhale.

OMG! OMG! Oh, my God!

This moment had just become the highlight of my career and I didn't quite know what to do with myself. I looked over at the other contestants and noticed that they were all in deep concentration working on their own models.

But they don't have a freakin' supermodel sitting in their chair!

Gathering myself together, I attempted to regain my composure and use the time to prep my tools and table, making sure that everything was pristine and perfect for my model's return. This was one of those occasions that was too much to take in all at once, but I knew that later when I looked back on this, I would smile to myself and tell anyone who was prepared to listen that I once did makeup for the hottest supermodel in the world.

Yikes! She's coming back! Get it together Willow! Stay calm. I told myself.

The Muse had changed into a pair of pink Repetto ballet pumps and was flashing her famous crooked smile as she walked towards me.

"Thank goodness for flat shoes! I always carry a spare pair in my bag just in case."

I smiled and indicated for her to look at my feet – we were both wearing the same shoes!

She smiled at me, "They're the best, aren't they?" Then she exhaled loudly before throwing herself up into the director's chair.

I finally got a grip and convinced myself she was just a woman from London who had worked hard and made it big in the fickle world of fashion.

"How do you do it?" I asked, as I purposefully smudged the eyeliner at the corner of her eye.

"Do what?"

"Keep it all together. How do you keep going when there's someone waiting to photograph you every second of the day?"

"Easy! Shades on, head down, and go, go, go!" she quipped while checking messages on her phone.

She flashed me a wicked smile, revealing the sharp incisors that she refused to tamper with. I had to admire her, in a world of Botoxed beauties with perfect teeth, she was a true stand out girl, supremely comfortable in her own skin. My admiration for her grew even more.

Twenty-five minutes later, an anticipatory hush swept over the crowd as Carlotta took to the podium to announce that there were only 5 minutes left of the competition. I surveyed the carefully defined features of my model's exquisite face; her eyes were closed but the almond-shaped outline of her upper eyelid had been carefully outlined in black liner. Her cupid lips were lined with red pencil and coloured in Dolce Vita by Dior; the stunning red that Isabella had used to showcase her artwork on Rick's bathroom mirror all those months ago. Even models like her had their imperfections, though. Her laughter lines were evidence of a life well-lived, and I quietly hoped that she would stay away from fillers and Botox; no amount of Botox should ever be allowed to blur those lines out.

Finally, Carlotta took the microphone in her hand and announced that the competition was over and that we had to put our brushes down. Adam Lambert was belting out "Superstar" on the store loudspeakers while Carlotta walked around each of the contestants, examining the makeovers and making notes in her pink leather agenda.

The atmosphere was strangely hushed, but the air seemed electrified by the collective anticipation. The other women had been itching to come over to my workstation to meet my model, but strangely for them they had stayed put at their stations, leaving *The Muse* and I to continue our chat. She was staring deep into the hand-held mirror, scrutinising every inch of her sculpted face. Personally, I thought I had done an amazing job but wasn't quite sure how she would react.

The Muse noticed that one side of the eyeliner looked a little wonky. Without thinking, she began to touch up the mistake.

Worried that Carlotta would notice, I knew that we were breaking the rules of the competition, but I couldn't quite find the strength to pluck up the courage to say anything to the world's top supermodel. I gritted my teeth in silence, hoping and praying that no-one would notice.

In a flash, my attention was caught by Lora from Saks who, unbeknownst to me, had been staring over at us this whole time.

Shit! If she says anything. — I'm out.

I looked back at Lora, silently begging her not to say anything as *The Muse* handed the pencil back to me.

That was when she realised in an instant the gravity of her actions.

"Oh no! I shouldn't have done that; you could be disqualified. Shit, I'm just so used to applying my own makeup…so sorry!"

I found myself in the very strange position of having to console my model while Carlotta stood only a few feet away talking to Lora and her model. I couldn't hear what they were saying instead, I studied their body language. Then all three turned to stare at *The Muse* and me.

"Sorry! I shouldn't have done that!" she said, her face filled with angst.

The Muse was changing out of her flat shoes into her Louboutin's in preparation for walking to the podium.

"Of course! Don't worry about it…it'll be fine, no one noticed!" I exclaimed knowing full well I was wearing the falsest smile on my face.

I hoped and prayed that she wouldn't see through my mask.

27

FLUSH

I watched *The Muse* saunter slowly and sexily towards the podium, hips swaying languidly to Frank Sinatra belting out 'New York, New York.' All eyes were firmly glued on her as she elegantly navigated her way through the rows and rows of makeup tables and contestants. It was as if no one else was in the room as her aura permeated through the ether. I felt a sense of motherly pride that she was my model, if only for this one afternoon.

It was as if all the tough times I had been through had magically disappeared in an instant. I was no longer that same troubled person, running from one disastrous situation to another; this time I had stayed to win the fight. No matter which way the competition turned out, I was proud of myself, perhaps for the first time in my life. I was truly proud of myself. I had navigated my way through a myriad of problems, dealt with far too many obstacles for one little person to deal with, and endured probably more than some would endure in a lifetime. Yet here I was, experiencing one of the most truly magical moments of my life.

There was nothing more for me to do. All my work was done. It was now up to the judges and the authorities to decide whether I got to remain in the country. I cleared my makeup table and stored my brushes in their canvas wrap. My trolley bag had been positioned under my table this whole time, now all I had to do was pack up the remainder of my belongings and I would be ready.

The action started with two uniformed from Homeland Security busting in through an open door and making their way towards Carlotta. They spoke for a few moments while Carlotta indicated for one of the perfume ladies to take the microphone from her. Carlotta looked over in my direction, then indicated to the guards my position on the beauty hall floor.

I felt like my feet were suctioned to the floor as they walked fast towards me. I knew I had failed the Green Card for Marriage interview and had expected this day to arrive, so it wasn't like they took me by surprise or anything, but still my feet would not move. Out of the corner of my eye, I saw The Muse stare at the men and then paled with relief as they focussed in on me instead.

"Are you Willow Campbell-Delgado?" the taller of the two asked, staring at me, then staring at a document he held in his hand.

"I am," I replied.

"Confirm your address for me please?" he asked.

"Would you like my permanent address or my temporary one?" I responded with such clarity of thought that took me by surprise.

The two officers turned to look at each other, confused by my accent and my response to their question.

"Permanent address, please."

The taller of the two adopted a stern approach but was caught in mid-sentence as another branch of Homeland Security officers invaded the beauty hall floor. I looked over to see that once again Carlotta was directing the crowd of maybe five men in my direction. Within seconds, I was surrounded by a barrage of men who were all staring at me. I noticed at that point that my model had made a swift disappearance and who could blame her?

But still, I stood with my feet stuck firmly to the floor as the officers talked amongst themselves, discussing what they were going to do with me.

Off to my right, a tall man stepped out of the audience of onlookers and he made his way towards the chief officer. His silhouette was unmistakable to me. It was Jackson.

What is he doing here? He's supposed to be undercover.

Jackson was talking in an animated fashion, while one by one he handed out what looked like blown-up black and white photographs to the bunch of guards standing next to me. I had no clue what was going on.

What's he up to? I wondered, trying in vain to see the photographs with my own eyes.

"Can I please see one of these photographs?" I asked a guard.

The guard handed me a photo. It was a wedding photograph, taken at Clements Estate in Loch Lomond.

Where the hell did he get those from?

Then he turned and stared at me, pointing in my direction as he spoke to the chief guard.

"So, as you can see from these images, this young lady really did love her husband and, in my opinion, she deserves to stay."

I was taken aback. Breathless. *He would do this for me?*

"She is innocent of any misdemeanour. She married Rick Delgado because she was in love with him. Her wedding was the real deal."

I looked at Jackson and at the crowd of onlookers who had moved closer. The crowd had gathered tightly around us. I was aghast, yet still my feet would not move. I was frozen to the spot.

"And who might you be?" the chief officer enquired as his underling ran a background check on Jackson.

"Jackson Dart. Real name Andrew McCullough. I defected here in 2011 from the cruise ship Gallant en route to the Galapagos Islands. I was one of the cruise ship dancers," he explained in a calm, matter-of-fact tone. He looked over at me and drew me a wry smile before handing over his paperwork.

Two guards approached Jackson and handcuffed him on the spot.

"Mr. McCulloch, you are under arrest for being an illegal immigrant in the USA. Come with us."

"Bloody hell! Leave him alone!" I shouted as a small circle of guards encroached on my space, indicating for me to remain quiet.

The guards marched Jackson out

I couldn't believe they were taking him away from me. I hurt inside. Real bad. *How can they do this? How could he make such a sacrifice for me?* No one had ever done anything like this for me. I began to cry. Real, hard gobby sobs erupted out of me.

"Leave him alone!" I shouted, feeling like I might be sick.

A half-hour later, I was sitting in a desolate Homeland Security office space, awaiting the arrival of an immigration lawyer. They offered me coffee, but I refused. I kicked the wheels of my trolley bag, the bag that contained the detritus of my life including a burgeoning collection of professional makeup supplies. Word filtered back to me that Isabella had signed off sick from the competition and that in her absence, I had won the Makeup Artistry Competition by default. But it all meant nothing to me now that they had taken Jackson away.

Each time an officer came into the room, I enquired to his whereabouts but was told in no uncertain terms that Jackson was in the process of being deported out of the country.

The thought trickled through my mind that I might also be huckled to the airport and put on the first departing flight to Glasgow.

"So, are they flying him to Dublin?" I enquired.

"I expect so," replied the officer. "All illegal aliens are deported back to the point of origin."

"But he left Ireland onboard a cruise ship. He didn't leave from an airport."

"Then they'll take him back to the port where he began his journey," said the officer.

"OK. Thanks," I stored the information away for future use.

Now, I knew where they were taking him; my black mood improved ever so slightly.

I worked out that Jackson had been illegal for eight years. That was a long time to be living on your nerves. I wondered if he felt a tad relieved that it was all over.

There was a stout knock at the door as the immigration lawyer, a tall woman in her early 40s entered the room accompanied by the chief Homeland Security officer. After polite introductions were made, the lawyer sat down opposite me.

"Have you been treated well?" she asked.

"Yes," I replied, not wanting to rock the boat

She brandished a collection of paperwork including the black and white wedding photographs that Jackson had gathered.

"Mrs. Campbell-Delgado, we have now spoken to your husband," she paused, "And after completing our background checks, we have decided that your marriage is indeed legitimate."

The lawyer stared at me, awaiting a reaction. But she did not get what she expected.

I stared back at her and said nothing. Inside I felt like my heart was breaking. It was breaking for Jackson.

"So, what happens now?" I asked, wiping a solitary tear off my cheek.

"You are free to go."

I stood up.

"Thank you," I said, while staring at my feet.

"I expect Mr. Delgado is waiting for you back at the apartment?" she asked.

"I expect he is," I replied, trying my best to look happy.

So, now I must return to Rick and make pretend like everything is OK? I thought. *For God's sake!*

28

BLUSH

Rick turned up to collect me. It was 8:30pm and raining. That's all I remember of that day. We had gone straight to an Italian roast house and sat on barstools facing out onto the street.

Rick was very apologetic about everything and we both concluded we had made a big mistake getting married so soon. We had got caught up on a romantic whim; caught up in the sweet romance of it all. If I were to be brutally honest, I had been looking for an escape and Rick had presented me with one. It had been hard to say no. Although part of me was pleased that I had been brave enough to say "yes" to his marriage proposal, I now know, looking back, we didn't really love each other. We agreed to put the episode in the past and to try to continue as friends. Rick would move onto the couch and I would have the bedroom. I would have to give up my independence temporarily, which meant I had to hand in my notice at the Hell's Kitchen apartment block.

We carried on with that arrangement for the next few months while I saved up for a deposit on a larger apartment. Rick didn't charge me for rent, out of guilt I think, but I wasn't in the position to question his motive. Suffice to say the arrangement worked well in the short term.

We had set a date for divorce proceedings to ensue after a year had passed. It all seemed very cold and calculating but deep in my heart, I knew it was for the best. It would be a release for both of us and the chance to eradicate a silly mistake. This arrangement came along with the surprising benefit of allowing me to regain a liking for Rick once more, although both Jackson and Jake were never far from my thoughts.

By early the following summer, I was firmly ensconced in my slightly larger Manhattan apartment in Hell's Kitchen. I had got to know the area rather well and enjoyed the proximity to the Hudson River. I had settled in well with my new colleagues at Barneys and I was preparing to take an Advanced Makeup Artistry certification at night school. I thought back to the conversation Jackson and I had that night in the dive bar when he had made me think hard about pursuing my dreams. He had been right all along. My success was down to me and to me alone...along with a sprinkling of fortitude.

The Muse and I had stayed in contact and she had even offered me the opportunity to be her personal makeup artist if ever I decided to go freelancing in London. For the first time in my life, I felt like I was making real progress. It was a very tempting offer, but it would mean leaving behind everything I had built up in New York...and I knew more than most that this town was not an easy town to make it in. It had a habit of chewing you up and spitting you out at the first opportunity.

As the days turned into weeks and the weeks turned into months, it wasn't long before I was offered a promotion to Lead Makeup Artist at Chanel and the opportunity to work backstage at New York Fashion Week.

It had been one year since Mrs. G had been indicted and she was due for release. The organisers had stuck up the proverbial two fingers at the authorities and had chosen to mark the occasion by seating Mrs. G in the front row of the February shows at Bryant Park. How fitting then that the woman who had given me my first opportunity to work in the city would now be witness to my progress at the shows.

As the shows began, the Chanel models paraded the housewares in true Chanel style. The prescribed makeup for the shows had been a mix of contemporary classic with a dash of futuristic flair – in other words, an almost impossible feat of makeup artistry was needed to pull off this daring look. I had hired Rose to be my first assistant, as one by one, we prepared and painted each elegant model who sat in the Chanel director's chair. Rose was beyond herself with excitement at the challenge she had been given, and by all accounts, she kept her cool and did well.

I, on the other hand, literally shook with fear until I managed to get a grip on myself. I told myself that all the challenges and hard knocks had been building up to this one amazing moment and that I deserved to be in this spot on this day. With my work done, and my models lined up ready to take to the stage in their finest Chanel garb, I took a breath as I saw Sandie Shaw take to the stage. There had been rumours that she would be singing live at the show, and there she stood in her trademark bare feet, surrounded by a sea of elegant, six-foot-tall models.

The opening chords to "Cool About You" by the Jesus and Mary Chain filled the tent as Sandie sang the words to one of my all-time favourite songs. The models took to the stage and struck a pose as I watched on with Rose at my side. Mrs. G and I exchanged a glance. I knew I had won her approval.

Later, as the shows wound down and the last remaining models had run off to attend the after-show parties that took place all around the city, I packed up the expensive arsenal of makeup tools and carefully put them away, secretly pleased with my accomplishment.

Just then, as I was about to leave, Rose called through to me, "Willow! There's some folks here to see you."

I glanced up to see Mrs. G enter the room, at her side stood Jake and a young blonde boy of perhaps eight or nine years old.

"Hello stranger!" I ran to Mrs. G and hugged her tightly while looking over her shoulder at Jake and the boy. As I parted from Mrs. G, Jake stood forward, "Willow, long time no see. There's someone you should meet." I looked down at the little boy, then back at Jake. He winked at me.

"Are you who I think you are?" I asked. The boy looked mystified.

"Dunno," he replied looking back at Jake for assistance.

"This is Billy," Jake beamed proudly.

I looked at Jake and Mrs. G.

"I heard through the grapevine about Billy and the extra work that Jake was doing to help out, so I made sure he got what he needed," Mrs. G offered. "Good to see you are doing such great work, Willow, keep it up."

"Oh, I will, don't you worry. I'm making some excellent contacts in the industry too," I said.

"I expect you are," she said. "Now I'll leave you lovebirds alone. I'm sure you've got a lot of catching up to do."

"Billy, come with me. There's some people I'd like you to meet," Mrs. G took Billy by the hand and led him out of the tent, leaving Jake and I alone for the first time in ages.

"That song she sang out there…did you pick it?" Jake asked, his eyes glinting under the harsh lighting of the backstage tent.

"No. But it is one of my favourites," I responded shyly.

"Cool," he said, staring at me, a second longer than necessary.

He offered his arm, "It's a nice day for a walk along the Hudson River." I accepted, smiled and prayed inwardly that he wouldn't take me for coffee at Gino's.

The End

In loving memory of my dad, Harry Burns,
who I spent the first twenty-one years of my life with.

"Give Peace a Chance"
John Lennon

ACKNOWLEDGEMENTS

Thank you to:

My 'Warpaint Warriors' who were always in the background urging me on to the finish line: My mum, Margaret, my brothers; Stephen and Craig, Helen, Susie Charleston Daisley, Toinette Campbell, Isabel Keenan, Denese Lovvorn, Tracy and Tommy McArthur, Liza Cortijo, Lorraine Steele, Marion Steele, Caroline Farry, Melanie Tyler, Jane McCormack, Laura Donnan, Lorna Doyle, Jackie Lavery, Janet Oetterer, Christian Linton and Vini Margalli.

My readers: Stacey Coyle, Danielle Keenan, Jackie Burns, Toni Burns, Charley Daisley, Kristine Humber, Karen Glen, Catherine Muir, Teresa Coleman, Joanne Lewis, Karen McDermott, Willis Middleton, Marilyn Anderson, Mary McKenzie and Hayley Myles.

The professionals: Editor - Amy Tipton of Feral Girl Books, Teresa Rodriguez - Editor-in-Chief, Haute Living San Francisco, Mayte Rodriguez Cedillo - Editor in Chief at Traveler Publications, Professor and TV writer - Ann Marie Di Mambro at Glasgow Caledonian University, Stephen McDermott - Book Cover Illustration, Anne McManus at Shed Media and Molly Bolt for encouraging me to write this book. The teachings of Napoleon Hill.

The soundtrack: Alicia Keys, Burt Bacharach, Karen Carpenter, The Mamas and Papas, The Jesus and Mary Chain and Primal Scream.

The family: Stevie, Joe and Jamie who's never faltering love for me and belief in me, made sure I finally finished this book.

Thanks for reading Warpaint! Please consider leaving a review at my J.J. Maya Author page on Amazon.

For updates on the sequel to Warpaint, subscribe here: https://mailchi.mp/55d48b70359c/jj-maya

CPSIA information can be obtained
at www.ICGtesting.com
Printed in the USA
BVHW030722070420
576992BV00006B/399